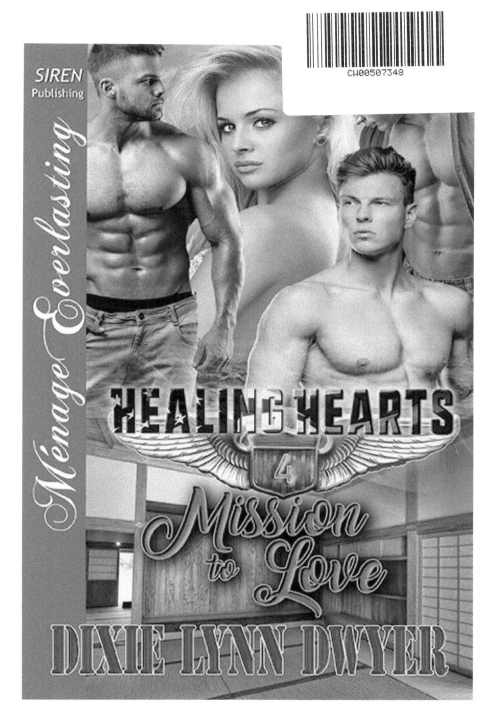

SIREN
Publishing

Ménage Everlasting

HEALING HEARTS

4

Mission
to Love

DIXIE LYNN DWYER

Healing Hearts 4: Mission to Love

April is hiding her true profession. She never lets down her guard and conditions herself to not need anyone to survive. Moving to Mercy changes her perspective on friendship and love, and she's willing to die to protect those she opened her heart to. It's a fine line between lying and protecting the three men she has fallen in love with. If she reveals her true profession, she puts them at risk. Plus they are Navy Seals and one is the Chief of Police.

Complicated doesn't begin to describe the situation. She may have to sacrifice the need and desire to be their woman in order to protect them from the current dangers of her career. Some things are meant to be, and the mission to take out terrorists and the ones responsible for killing agents and Seals, may turn into a mission to save their love and validate that nothing will stand in the way of their destiny.

Genre: Contemporary, Ménage a Trois/Quatre, Romantic Suspense
Length: 43,472 words

HEALING HEARTS 4: MISSION TO LOVE

Dixie Lynn Dwyer

Siren Publishing, Inc.
www.SirenPublishing.com

DEDICATION

Dear readers,

Thank you for purchasing this legal copy of *Mission to Love*.

April is a secret agent. Capable of things not many would understand. Her profession has kept her from opening up her heart and she's okay with that, accepting to that. Until she meets three SEALS. She falls in love and of course doesn't quite know how to handle it, and neither do they. It's a recipe for disaster, but the desire, the attraction, the lust is so incredibly strong none of them can resist. The result? Chaos, secret missions, gunfire, explosions, and a plethora of danger that will take one capable blonde spy, several soldiers, a colonel, and three very special SEALS to win another one for the good guys.

May you enjoy April's journey, and get ready for a heck of a ride.

Happy reading,

HUGS!

Dixie

For all titles by Dixie Lynn Dwyer, please visit
www.bookstrand.com/dixie-lynn-dwyer

Healing Hearts 4: Mission to Love

DIXIE LYNN DWYER
Copyright © 2018

Prologue

"I want those shipments. I don't care who has to die. Get them from that holding facility. It's in the middle of nowhere."

"Now is not the time to draw attention to any of us, Kerrin. I can get you more weapons, drugs, women, whatever the fuck you need," Rosen Armique said calmly over the phone, but he really wasn't feeling so calm. He didn't like how things went down a month ago, how Wegman wound up dead by federal agents and some military special forces guys, nor the buzz he picked up on around some of the businesses Rosen was a silent partner in. He needed to be cautious and to calm Kerrin down before he did something stupid and got them all busted. It was a tricky situation. Kerrin was into crazy shit, including providing women for clients negotiating money deals in and out of the US. Rosen saw it as a lucrative business, as well, and was working with a few trusted men to get in on this business. It seemed to him that the trickiest part was getting the women out of the country. Once they did that, it was clear sailing. Investigators wouldn't risk or waste manpower at that point. He had ideas, and with Victoria's help, this could be quite profitable and his own hands wouldn't need to get dirty.

"I have very powerful, important clients coming in every weekend for the next several months. They have particular tastes, and one coming in this weekend enjoys being surrounded by beautiful women. There are six others accompanying them, and each of those individuals have particular tastes. Now in order to appease him, my gifts were those weapons that are stored at the warehouse, some additional drugs for their entertainment, and of course women. I need guns and drugs yesterday, Rosen."

"Not a problem. Just stay clear of that warehouse, will you? I have some plans in motion, and believe me, we'll be pocketing so much money that one warehouse won't faze us at all."

"I hope so. When will I get what I need?"

Rosen looked at his watch and then at Gorbin and Fulta, his main guys. "My men will have it delivered by tomorrow afternoon."

"Very well. I heeded your advice, Rosen. I hope that you will soon come to one of the events at my estate."

"I look forward to it in the near future." He ended the call and then explained the situation.

"We'll take care of it, Rosen. You also need to call Victoria back," Gorbin told him.

"Why is that?"

"She has information for you on one of the individuals who was behind that raid and Wegman's death."

"I'm not sure I really care at this point. I think I need to cut my losses."

"She said you would be interested to know," Gorbin added. Rosen squinted and nodded.

"Take care of that for me, and let me know when it's done and delivered. I'll call her now."

The other two men exited the room, and Rosen exhaled and then called Victoria.

"Hello, Victoria."

"Rosen, I take it you've heard from Kerrin."

"Indeed, and everything is going to work out fine, thanks to you of course," he complimented. Victoria was an exceptional woman. Besides her incredible and successful businesses, she was combat trained and a survivor of military bombings and takeovers in her home country of Syria. She had a deep hatred for Americans, especially soldiers. She was a crucial asset to gathering women across the world to satisfy specific orders of wealthy businessmen.

"You know I come through for you every time. However, I haven't gotten any personal requests from you," she said, flirting with him.

"I've been busy."

"I've got some gorgeous young ones ripe for the taking just in from Madrid."

"I appreciate the offer."

"You could always use one of my secret locations if you have your own toy in mind and want to bring her. Just say the word. It's the least I could do for such a close friend like you."

He knew she wanted to sleep with him, but he didn't want or need complications. And the woman was a dominatrix, and that wasn't his thing. He was the one who dominated.

"I'll keep that in mind. I'm a bit busy with business dealings."

"Which leads me to why I wanted to talk to you, Rosen. I got the confirmation I was waiting on. A certain agent you despise was right there in the middle of the action. In fact, he seemed to initiate the investigation into Vince and that small-time idiot, Cavanaugh. To think that a nobody caused such destruction is almost laughable."

"Well, I'm not laughing, nor are any of our associates considering that over five hundred thousand in merchandise is now under the protected of the US military," Rosen replied and thought about this a moment.

"I'm working on retrieving that supply. With time, security will be less and less, and then there will be opportunity to make the move. You don't need to worry. As I mentioned, I have people who can handle it, so your hands and mine remain clean. I say we take this agent out. Him and the organization he works for have been nothing but a thorn in some of our associate's sides. They're clamming up, fearful of taking chances on orders. That's bad for business."

"So is killing government agents."

"So you want to ignore this, and just hope his pursuit ended with Vince and Cavanaugh?"

"For now, unless there's indication that they haven't given up and are still sniffing around. Let this all blow over, and when he least expects anything, when he's comfortable and maybe living his personal life, then we strike."

"Ahhh, like maybe when he takes a little vacation, or is out partying with friends he gets into an accident?"

"Something like that, or perhaps he can be of use to us to hold on to in order to entice some of his associates so they can be eliminated, as well. I hate to assume anything or make premature plans. I assume you have someone on him?"

"Yes, and he is discreet and very in tune to the environment he works in. If there is more info to get, he'll get it."

"Very well then. Let's go on with business as usual. Be sure you pick some very special women for this next delivery. Kerrin is being so particular."

"Tell me about it. Virgins are hard to come by these days, just as voluptuous women with emerald-green eyes, and what is with women that resist more? What happened to liking a weak woman, a damsel in distress, or one dominated by restraints?" she said to him. He chuckled. She knew his tastes. It had been a while, the last one nearly a year ago. It was a shame she died so soon.

"It's always interesting to have a woman who will do her best to resist. There are a few businessmen who will definitely be placing their own orders after getting a taste. Keep me posted on the other situation."

"Of course. Talk to you soon, Rosen."

He ended the call and leaned back in his chair. So Agent Mike Waters was a potential thorn in his side that needed to be plucked. The agents had been a problem since the incident in Syria. Fucking Navy Seals. In the future they needed to be more careful. This new shipment should go off without any problems. He smiled. It would all work out, and if Agent Waters was still snooping, then he would be eliminated sooner than later.

Chapter One

April Marris sat on the bench looking out at the water. She had strolled through the town of Mercy, deciding to have her morning coffee after a long jog along the streets. When she sat down and exhaled, her heart was heavy. Especially as she saw the police patrol car doing regular rounds and then the scene unfold before her. The officer got out of the car and went toward a young woman and her little girl. He bent down, and the little girl hugged him tight. The mom smiled, and April knew that they were a couple. When he stood up with the little girl clinging to him and hugged and kissed his wife who smiled and looked so in love, April felt the tears reach her eyes.

Looking back toward the water, she recalled that day in early April when her dad, a police officer, left for work. He smiled, gave her a kiss and a hug goodbye, and told her to be a good girl and take care of Mommy. She always found that funny, giggling as if she weren't capable of taking care of Mommy, that Mommy took care of her. She had no idea that it would be the last time she hugged her daddy. The last time she got to feel his big strong arms around her or inhale his cologne and feel so loved.

Tears filled her eyes, and she submerged them. *God, it's been so many years.*

She closed up after that. Never really feeling or being affected by much, and always keeping up a bit of a wall. She figured in doing so, it would hurt less when things didn't work out, or if something went wrong. Not even when she met Evan, a Navy Seal, had she allowed herself to take a chance with him. She had a feeling it may be only sex when she did cave in to his flirtatious actions, but it never happened. She fought and resisted, making out with him then ending things before they wound up in bed. All her excuses of their paths crossing in their professions, or causing problems with jealousy or other things when she would need to lie about where she was going for weeks at a time, just like Evan would when he went on a mission at a moment's notice.

By keeping that small wall around her heart out of fear, she never felt anything to her core, to deep within a heart that felt broken and incapable of loving. The few intimate relationships she had failed. Not because the men didn't love her or treated her badly, but because she felt incapable of love. She feared it and held back, and it caused her nothing but problems. It was easier to be alone. To train and train and train until she was exhausted from training.

When she entered the police academy, there wasn't one thing that she didn't conquer, nor one aspect she didn't shine on. She did the same testing any man did, and she excelled in it. Her determination to get as much training as possible was her motivation so she could take men like the cop killer who killed her father and four others off the streets. Her biggest achievement aside from the position she held today was the sweet revenge she achieved, using her connections, her abilities and brain to capture and bring justice for her father and the other victims' families when she found their killer. It was nearly twenty years later, but she did it.

She had thought the day Emanuel Pheldman was arrested would have brought her complete closure. But it hadn't. She had become too far desensitized to feeling emotions, and it became a bittersweet moment that came and went as quickly as one case after another. When her mother passed, it only hardened her heart even more so. She had no family, and friends were few and far between because work and achieving the next goal, the next big thing, were her focus. What that hard work ethic and obsession did do was cause higher-ups to take notice of her and then to approach her on this position. A combination of training from CIA, FBI, military, and law enforcement. She conquered every aspect. She was a borderline spy, but a domestic one at that.

To top it off, Evan died while being part of a rescue operation that also involved her and other agents. The sadness would have been ten times worse if they had been lovers. It solidified the fact that she didn't need to date anyone in law enforcement, in the military or anything associated with it. That left her affairs to one stockbroker, one lawyer, and a doctor. All as obsessed with their professions as she was with hers, which left their relationships falling apart and solely existing for quick sex to ease their aches and nothing deeper. She was done with all of that.

She took a sip of her coffee. Her mind wandering from one thing to the next. Her father, her career, the fact she nearly died in a damn boat on the Cypress near Syria, and coming here thinking settling down was what she wanted, but she wound up saving Amelia's life and killing that piece of shit Turbin once and for all.

Now that just opened a can of worms. She snickered. No one but Pierre knew it was her. Well, Mike figured it out. She exhaled and grinned. Mike. He showed up at Corporal's and hung with her and some of her friends. She was grateful because Caden, Simon, and Aqua couldn't seem to take their eyes off of her, and she was affected by them. She didn't want to face that. She knew it was a waste of time. She didn't do relationships, and surely she shouldn't entertain one with three Navy Seals, and one chief of police to boot. Not after her history with men like that and knowing Caden. Simon, and Aqua were like Evan, and perhaps they even knew him. She didn't want to think about that possibility. But damn were they three of the sexiest men she'd ever laid eyes on. She could see herself letting go with them, and maybe that was what scared her the most. Her friend Karen told her she was a love-them-and-leave-them woman, and there wasn't a thing wrong with that. Sex was important and helped to release tension and to feel human when their jobs and actions seemed more robotic than human. April didn't think it was worth the aggravation and didn't quite agree with Karen, especially considering Karen was on her fourth husband and more than likely it wouldn't last. She hadn't spoken to her in over a year's time.

She took a few more sips of coffee and stretched out her legs. The jog had been long and tiresome. A few more minutes of rest and she would run back toward her place on the beach.

Something made her turn to the left, and she was shocked at her reaction to seeing the chief of police, Caden Farmer, getting out of his patrol truck.

She looked away as he looked toward her, and she hoped that he hadn't stopped just to talk to her. Then part of her felt giddy if he did in fact stop to talk to her. The attraction was there, but given her line of work and the secrets she held, she couldn't exactly entertain the fling. She looked back toward the water. Then suddenly she felt self-conscious about what she was wearing. A tight-fitting sports top that accentuated her very large breasts. Wasn't much she could do about that. Her short jogging shorts exposed her long, tanned legs, and her long, blonde hair was pulled back and up with a running cap, also protecting her eyes from the sun.

She felt guilty, like she shouldn't talk to him, have feelings for him, especially because of what she did only two weeks ago. She remembered what he looked like dressed in black military gear along with his brothers, Aqua and Simon. They were ready to get Turbin, but she took him out. How could she ever tell them who she really was? This was something she faced for years now. They wouldn't be a simple pleasure and then she could move on. Mercy was different. Mercy was where ménage relationships shined and people retired, settled down, and had lives together. She didn't think she was capable of that at all.

"Morning, April."

His deep, sexy voice immediately hit her heart and her pussy somehow. She was shocked. She even placed her hand over her belly, pretending that she was shocked to see him and that he surprised her. She knew he was coming. She was so well trained.

She looked up toward him, blocking the sun from her eyes despite the cap she wore, by holding her hand over them. He looked so good. He wore his hat, those dark sunglasses where she couldn't see his eyes. She wondered if he were looking her over because she suddenly felt aroused and every part of her reacted. She was looking him over, too. The tight uniform shirt against thick, bulging muscles was a turn-on. The uniform, the gun, the fact he was a Seal was sexy, and she was certain women threw themselves at him and his brothers all the time. The thought annoyed her. She kept her cool though. It had taken years to have a shielded heart, and she wasn't faltering now.

"Morning, Chief," she said, and he shook his head. He looked around them, with his hands on his hips, and she seemed to have pissed him off somehow.

She stood up so she wouldn't hurt her neck so much staring up at the man. She tossed her coffee cup in the garbage by the bench. Even standing, he was way taller than her. He had to be about six feet four. She was five feet six. He yanked off his sunglasses, and those bold blue eyes of his held hers as he stared down into her eyes, appearing pissed off. "I thought we discussed the whole name thing."

He was fuming mad, and she knew why. As he and his brothers tried to flirt with her, touch her at the bar the other night, she used Mike and his friends as a way to throw Caden and his brothers off. She couldn't believe how attracted she felt, and Mike played along, allowing her to hug him and kiss his neck. He was a gentleman, though, and didn't caress her ass or anything, just rubbed her back and kissed her neck back and whispered to her asking if she was okay and who was she trying to avoid? Thank God Mike hadn't pushed for information.

Caden licked his lips, and she nearly moaned she was so affected by him.

"Caden, remember?"

"I'm just being respectful. What's wrong with you? You seem agitated. Rough morning in Mercy?" she instigated and didn't know why. She just felt compelled to ruffle his feathers even though it was asking for trouble.

She hadn't expected him to wrap his arm around her waist and pull her close either. She gasped. His other hand came up and cupped her cheek, tilting her chin up toward him.

"You know how to get under my skin like no other. Don't know what games you're playing, why you're denying the attraction, but I don't expect this nonsense to continue much longer. Myself, Simon, and Aqua aren't patient men." She felt his hand slid along her hip and then over her ass, giving it a tap. He pulled back, and her face must have given away her shock as he tipped his hat at her.

"Have a good day, April, and next time I see you, I expect a warm welcome." He walked away, his radio going off, and she was numb with emotions she didn't want to digest. Hot damn was the chief a piece of work. Maybe it wouldn't be so bad to engage in a little get-to-know-ya action after all.

She glanced at her watch as she watched him drive away. She needed to get home to shower and then do some work on the computer for Pierre. Another case, some more intel, and perhaps a trip to New York by the end of the week for business. She set her watch and then took off jogging. She didn't want to leave this town, not even for weekends or a few days to aid in investigations for the special unit she was a part of. She didn't want to go back full-time either and be in the field, working undercover or risking her neck on the line unless it was necessary. No, she liked pretending to be normal, when she was anything but normal. A trained killer, a spy of sorts, a woman who would never be able to live a normal life like her friends did, ever again. She couldn't stand to be bored and sit around either. She was long past recovering from her gunshot wounds, long past the mission gone wrong, and was perfectly fine jumping in to aid when her abilities and expertise was needed. More of a freelance position than steady. If she went back steady, then the higher-ups would think she was back in the game, and she didn't think she wanted to do that anymore. Mostly because of Mercy and the friends she made here, and also because of Caden, Simon, and Aqua. If she were to entertain this attraction, then she would need to do so with a clean conscience.

She focused on her jog and not the complications of this town and the men she desired. She just couldn't let down her guard, and the case wasn't complete. Not by a long shot and not until Rosen Armique and his group of associates were captured or killed.

* * * *

Amelia was shaking, crying, and trying to wipe her eyes.

"Easy now. It's going to be okay. You don't have to push so hard, Amelia. Therapy takes time," Ice told her.

She took the tissue he offered and wiped her eyes. "I want to get better faster. For Watson, Dell, and Fogerty. One minute I'm fine, and then I'm not."

"You're trying to rush things. What you went through was emotionally traumatic, and that alone could truly make you feel scared of even the everyday things. Add in what Cavanaugh put you through on a regular basis, and of course it's worse. But it is normal to not feel safe being alone. Have you spoken to the men about it?"

She shook her head.

"Because?"

She looked at him with tears in her eyes. "I don't want to be weak. They're so strong. Their jobs, the things they experienced require them to be tough physically and emotionally. They won't want a woman so weak and fragile. One that starts to panic when I'm alone even just to shower, or to do laundry. I can't explain it. When I'm alone I feel vulnerable, and weak. Like I can't protect myself. Then I get angry for being so weak and I think I'm completely reliant on them, and that isn't healthy."

"I understand what you're saying, and with time the fears and weakness will get less and less."

"No. No, I don't want to hear about time healing me, Ice. I don't. I need to do something."

He exhaled and licked his lip. "How do you spend your days?"

She stared at him. She thought about it. One of the guys was always in the house with her, but they were busy working and doing things, so she sat around a lot and thought.

"You need to get busy doing other things than sitting around and thinking, letting your mind wander over the bad stuff. You have a new life now, Amelia. Cavanaugh is dead. He can't hurt you ever again. His words, his actions are gone. This is your life, your new start. You have three strong, caring men who love you deeply. They'll support you and help you in every way they can. You have your friends, too. Make some plans. I've heard that the Y offers some great self-defense training and kickboxing courses. What about a physical activity that gets you moving, and also could give you the confidence to feel stronger and more capable instead of feeling dependent to the point of being depressed?"

"I've thought about it. Casey has been going, and she told me yesterday how much fun it is. That the instructors are nice and all, but—" She stopped and thought about it. She hadn't been going out anywhere without her men.

"What is it?"

"I haven't gone out anywhere really, and when I do I always have Watson, Dell, or Fogerty with me. I think they would tell me that they would teach me things, you know, so I wouldn't be so fearful."

He nodded. "I'm certain they could, but perhaps part of the therapy of this is doing it on your own. Gaining some control of your life, of the fears of going solo. The danger is over. You need to be your own person."

"That's the thing. I get what you are saying. I can feel myself losing control, and I don't like it. I know it, and I can't stop it."

"What do you mean?"

"I mean I let them make the decisions. I give in to whatever they want because I don't want to disagree or have conflict. Even over stupid things like what to have for dinner or what to watch on TV or a drink to have, I don't know, just stupid stuff."

"Getting out of your comfort zone is going to take time, but you need to remember that with Watson, Dell, and Fogerty, it's different. They're your support network, your boyfriends who love you and would do anything for you, so there's no need to feel like you need to appease them. It will cause problems later. Perhaps talking to them about it may help."

She smirked. "If I tell them about this, then they will go out of their way to make sure decisions I make are based on my wants and desires and not theirs."

"Well then, try to make the decisions you want. Even the littlest things will help when the bigger ones come along."

"Okay."

"So you'll think about venturing out, maybe some self-defense?"

"Maybe. I did hear from April, and she wanted to get together for lunch. She suggested she could come by the house. Do you think I should go out instead?"

He smiled. "I think the decision is yours, and you need to make it without overthinking."

"Hmm, I'm going to have a hard time doing something so simple."

"It's normal though. Remember that anyone who has had such traumatic experiences as you have go through similar things. It's a process of gaining back control and you can do it. I know you can."

She smiled. "Thanks, Ice." As they ended the session and stood up, she looked into the mirror to make sure her makeup wasn't a mess. Fogerty was waiting for her, and he would notice and get upset.

"How is Casey doing? I haven't seen her at Corporal's too much."

She gave a soft smile. It seemed that Ice often asked about Casey, yet he really didn't know her. He, like many, just knew her as the woman whose boyfriend shot up the place, shot her, and that Kai disarmed.

"She has a hard time going to Corporal's and usually doesn't stay long. She won't go down that hallway by the bathroom. It's tough for her."

"I could imagine," he said, looking concerned.

"If I go to Corporal's Friday I'm going to ask her to come along. If you're not busy, you should come."

"I'll see. My brothers may have some plans already," he told her.

"Okay," she said.

He opened the door, and there was Fogerty, his expression guarded until he looked her over as if making sure she was in one piece. Then he exhaled as he pulled her into his arms and hugged her.

"Okay, sweetie?" he asked.

"Yes, Fogerty," she whispered, and then he shook Ice's hand.

"See you next week," Ice said, and they headed out.

* * * *

Fogerty couldn't help the uneasy feeling he had every time Amelia went to therapy. He just didn't want her feeling any more pain or sadness. He hated seeing tears in her eyes, and yet he knew that Ice would help her. He just wished there was more he could do for her.

Fogerty held her close as they walked.

"So, lunch out, maybe at Sully's by the marina?" he asked, and felt her tighten up. She cleared her throat, and he stopped, cupped her cheek, and stared down into her eyes.

"We don't have to," he whispered, trying to read her. He knew she was scared all the time. That she hated being alone. She tried hiding it from them, but when they appeared, they could each see the trepidation on her face and then the tears.

She closed her eyes and took a deep breath and exhaled. She gave a soft smile. "Sure," she said, her voice cracking. He squinted.

"Really? I mean if you don't want to."

"No, we should. What about Dell and Watson? Could they meet us?" she asked. He smiled and pressed his lips to hers. He kissed her until she was limp in his arms, and he thought that skipping lunch and taking her home to bed would be so much better. She needed to do this. Something happened in therapy today, he just knew it. He slowly released her lips, and she held on to him, then hugged him tight.

"I love you so much, Fogerty. I don't want to be a burden. I want to try to be strong," she said, and he caressed her hair and her back.

"You're the bravest, strongest woman I know, sweetie. I'm here for you always." When he pulled back, tears were in her eyes, but she was smiling wide.

"Hmm, you're so beautiful." He stroked her cheek.

She nibbled her bottom lip.

"We'll call the others on the way," he said, and they headed to the truck.

Amelia heard her cell phone ring and glanced down at it. "It's April," she said and answered the phone.

"Hi, April."

"Hey, sweetie, how was therapy?"

"Good." She said felt the lump in her throat. April had been so supportive of her. She particularly remembered the night at Corporal's when Amelia pretended to hate Fogerty and his brothers and want nothing to do with them. April hadn't asked any questions. She just supported her and even walked her out. It was like she understood what happened. It made her also think about April's own experiences and wonder more about her.

"I was wondering if you wanted to meet up for lunch tomorrow?"

"Uhm, I'm not sure."

"If you don't feel comfortable going out yet, then I can come to you, or you can come over to my house and bring the guys. It's no problem."

"Can I let you know later? I'm actually going to Sully's with Fogerty and maybe Dell and Watson, too. Fogerty is calling them now."

"Really? That's fantastic."

"Well, don't celebrate anything yet. I'm shaking like a leaf." She reached out to hold on to Fogerty's leg, as he was talking to one of the guys while driving. He glanced at her and winked, and she smiled then leaned against him.

"Okay, you enjoy yourself, and we'll talk later."

"Okay, so we'll meet you there in fifteen minutes," Fogerty said into his phone, and Amelia smiled. She could do this, especially with her men around. With them she could do anything.

Chapter Two

"What do you have, Vince?" Mike asked, looking over the file he handed him.

"That situation with Cavanaugh and Turbin really opened up a slew of information. We've been checking out some of the people who were in that room dining and doing the sexual acts. Turns out that Turbin had the connections. A slew of those women were forced sex slaves originally from other countries but shipped to Syria and Kuwait of all places. Some of them were willing to be sex slaves in order to receive money for their poor families. It's sick, but also sent up additional red flags considering that some of the men detained were businessmen involved in imports and exports as well as banking overseas."

"We should be very careful how much we dig. Could be that some of these businessmen are the money backers to Turbin's business or maybe even buyers for the guns deal Cavanaugh was negotiating with Turbin. This case is getting bigger and bigger," Mike said.

"More and more complicated, as well. Heard that Colonel Brothers is now involved deeper and really wanting to capture all responsible for getting those Seals killed and the other soldiers along the way that were killed."

"I don't blame him, Vince. I want that, too. I'm going to transfer this stuff to my connection. See what pops up so we can connect the dots."

"No problem. We'll keep digging quietly," Vince added and then left the room.

Mike took out the nontraceable phone and called April.

* * * *

"Mike, this is heavy stuff, and there is definitely a connection to the case Colonel Brothers and our team are working on. You're going to have to be sure that Vince doesn't dig too much."

"I already explained things to him. Between you and I, I don't like the whole sex slave business being in the middle of guns and terrorist activities, but I guess it comes with the territory. We need to identify the money backers. They have to meet somehow and negotiate."

"Perhaps over some sex dinner party like the one at the hotel. Maybe they talk, make deals, and then engage in sexual fantasy playing. We've seen it before."

"Oh, yes we have, and I remember one case you were on and had to go in undercover."

"Don't remind me. I wasn't exactly thrilled to have the .22 between my legs, never mind such a small weapon against such big men."

"You did it though. Pulled that right out from under that sexy dress with the lace peeking out by your breasts. The slit in that dress was so high when you turned the swell of your—"

"Enough, Mike. I was undercover."

"You were the fantasy in every man's dream in the agency," he added.

"You're such an idiot."

He laughed. "On a lighter note, I really need you."

"What?"

"I need a date this Friday and only for about three hours," Mike said to April over the phone. She had been typing away on the computer, finishing up some information to send to Pierre.

She leaned back and chuckled.

"Seriously? For what?" she asked him.

"Dinner party at Carlyl's. Black tie, cocktail dress, great food, and I have to have a date, or I'll look like a total loser in front of all those blue suits and Cynthia Longing."

She laughed. "Cynthia dropped you like a hot potato and moved on pretty quickly if I recall. She still with Edward?"

"That dick thinks he's such a big shot. He fucking sells jewelry."

"He's loaded, Mike."

"What happened to money not meaning everything to a good woman?"

"Well, first you have to be dealing with a good woman. If I recall correctly, you picked her up at a bar, and when she asked you what you did for a living you told her you could tell her but then you'd have to kill her." He laughed.

"You saw her body?"

"Please," she said.

"It worked."

"For sex, but nothing more. She realized you were in law enforcement and the dollar signs she saw disappeared and so did she."

"She pissed me off so much."

"Forget about her."

"They're going to be there. Her and Edward, and you are like super fucking hot. It's a fundraiser for officers shot in the line of duty. Come on, you're going anyway."

"I was only going for a little while. I'm supposed to go to Corporal's to meet my friends."

"You can go afterwards. Three hours. Just enough time to make that bitch suffer."

She exhaled. "Fine, but I'm seriously leaving when I want to."

"Yes! I'll pick you up at seven."

"I'll meet you there at seven." She ended the call and then smiled. He was such a character, but he truly did not have one commitment bone in his body. A sexy body at that, but not her type at all and just a friend. With those thoughts, she thought about the chief and his brothers. Damn were they fantasies. All those muscles and capabilities. The only way to avoid doing something stupid was to stay clear of them.

Her phone rang again, and this time it was Pierre.

"Hi, Pierre what's up?"

"A lot."

"Oh no, what?"

"That info you found out on a chartered plane in Syria? Its passengers are various businessmen. Men who have some connections to Kerrin Bulla. Remember him?"

"Yeah, of course I do, and he was the right person to keep eyes on despite the agency thinking otherwise."

"Well, now we know why. Those agents were working for the bad guys, for Rosen, not us. You found that out the hard way, and it nearly cost losing you besides over a dozen agents and military soldiers."

"Shit, this is leading back to what we were originally on a year ago."

"I'm going to put Mike on alert. He's going to be assigned to one of the investigations as we go and assign others. There were about six businessmen that need looking into."

"I know that him and Vince came up with connections to men at the hotel in the dining room with the sex slaves. We both know that Turbin was into that business as well as abducting women. Perhaps these businessmen are dealing with Kerrin. Remember what I said about Rosen connecting to Kerrin if they aren't already partners in business?"

"Wess and Cole knocked that idea of yours down. Who would have known they were working against us and working for Rosen?" Pierre said.

"No one did, and it caused a lot of people to get hurt and relationships destroyed out of distrust and fear that there were more rats."

"Worse of all was you being caught in the middle and nearly dying."

"What will you need from me?" she asked, changing the direction of this conversation back to the business at hand. Pierre was silent a moment.

"Not anything right now. That trip to New York may come Monday, so enjoy the evening with Mike Friday," he said, and she was shocked.

"How did you…? Wait, he literally just called me."

"I spoke to him earlier and gave him the heads-up on things. I mentioned you going Friday. I know the cause is dear to your heart."

"Hmm, you know we're just going as friends so he can piss off that woman Cynthia."

"With you as his date, that will surely happen. He's a good guy."

"Don't go there. You know we are just friends."

"So that town getting to you, softening you up?"

"What?"

"I don't know, maybe you're more interested in the chief and his brothers? Navy Seals did help you out a time or two."

"Very funny."

"We checked them out. I know you did, as well. Quite impressive men, and I'm sure you saw that they were good friends with the Seals that died in Syria."

"I know that, which makes things complicated."

"Not really."

"How can you say 'not really'? It would be disastrous. They were probably friends with Evan. You think after that, even though Evan and I were just seeing one another, that I would consider anyone even remotely close to law enforcement or military? Not going to happen."

"Dating wealthy men in business or the medical field didn't work out either. You can't help who you're attracted to. Besides, you've got time on your hands, unless you were lying about the freelance work and want back in full time? I know the commanders will be fighting over you."

"Very funny, and no, I'll stick to what I'm doing. Besides, you saw their records, and you can figure out their personalities. They would not accept a woman of my capabilities. They want to be in charge. They are dominant, bossy, commanding, and seem to be controlling, as well. We would clash heads."

"Not necessarily. You never let go. They could be the ones to help you do that."

"Okay, Dr. Phil, don't quit your day job. Let's get back to business."

"I share things with you."

She exhaled.

"Okay, okay, back to business. I'll send over the list of names. Discreetly, find out what you can on their businesses and their connections to Kerrin. Oh, and how is Amelia doing? I meant to ask."

"She sounded good when I spoke to her earlier. We're meeting for lunch tomorrow."

"Without her men?"

She snickered. "No, with them nearby. She's also supposed to try a self-defense class with Casey tonight."

"Wow, sounds like Ice is helping her out, and she's determined to feel stronger."

"Maybe pushing herself a bit much."

"She's a good friend. I know you care a lot about all your friends you've made there. I'm glad Mercy is working out, but we do miss you in the field."

"Yeah, well, not quite ready to get shot at."

"You healed quickly."

"Not wanting to talk about it."

"Okay, enjoy and let me know how it works out."

She ended the call and sighed. Another thing she needed to worry about were the two bullet wounds she sported on her body. One right in her chest, making sexy clothing a little difficult to find, and one in her side right above her hip bone. Thank god it hadn't hit her hip bone, or it would have shattered and she more than likely would have been in a wheelchair if not dead. She exhaled. She had a story all made up for the scars though. A teenage tragedy living in the tough neighborhoods of NY and those damn drive-by shootings. She was lucky to survive.

She felt guilty about that, but she had no choice. If she were ever intimate with a man again, then she would need the lie to help cover her real profession. This job sucked the life out of her, and any hope of normalcy.

* * * *

Aqua was walking through the supermarket grabbing some things they needed at home when he heard the deep voice. He didn't know why he even bothered to look, but the way the man complimented the woman, telling her she was the prettiest thing he had ever seen and that his brother thought so, too, snagged Aqua's attention. What he hadn't expected to see was April, standing by the aisle, hands on the cart and smirking. The two men were invading her space, their hands on her cart, and they weren't giving up on her.

She looked good as usual. Sporting a pair of low-riding jeans, heeled sandals, and a V-neck top that accentuated her large breasts immediately drew his eyes to her every curve. Her long blonde hair was pulled back in a low bun at the back of her head with tendrils of hair falling in a sexy manner done on purpose. He couldn't see her gorgeous emerald-green eyes from here, but he knew how mesmerizing they were. It pissed him off that those men were hitting on her, just like it pissed him off as men hit on her at Corporal's. He thought about her and Mike, wondering if they were more than friends or if she was playing that up the other night to get him and his brothers to think she was involved with him. His gut turned with anger and jealousy.

"You have a full cart. Bet they'll be a lot of bags to carry out to your car. We can help you with that," the other guy said, and she exhaled. He hoped she didn't flirt back. He didn't know why he was even standing there except for the fact that this woman got to him and his brothers. To Caden especially quickly.

"Now, fellas, I appreciate the compliments, truly I do, but you're wasting your time. I'm not interested. It's been a long day, and if you'll excuse me, I need to finish up." She went to move, and the big guy got in her way. Aqua instantly got annoyed. Before this turned into something bad, he cleared his throat.

"Hey, babe, I couldn't find that cereal you like," he said and walked right up behind her, placed his milk and eggs into her cart, and then wrapped his arm around her waist. He gave the two men an expression that should warn them to take a hike.

"Who are you?" the one guy asked.

Aqua kept a hand on her hip and stepped to the side. "Do you want to know, or perhaps you need to run along now and go sniffing elsewhere?" he said firmly and felt April tighten up. Luckily the two men must have seen the look in Aqua's eyes as they gave her a nod and another look over before they slowly walked away. They didn't go far though, so he slid back behind her, moved his hand under her top, along her belly and waist, pulling her back against his front before leaning forward to kiss her neck. She smelled so good, and fit against him perfectly. She was feminine, muscular, and he was completely turned on by her.

"What do you think you're doing?" she whispered, her voice catching in her throat.

"Getting rid of the trash, sweetheart. I'd better stay close. Those men look stubborn." He slid his hand away from her waist and over her ass before he met her gaze with his. She stared up at him with those gorgeous emerald-green eyes like no others he had ever seen. She was stunning, and goddamn did she fill out a pair of tight blue jeans like no one else. The hem of her T-shirt, a pale pink, lifted slightly, revealing her skin and trim waist, and the top dipped just slightly but she was well endowed and then some. He had felt her muscular abs just now as he held her close. The woman could be on the cover of a workout magazine.

"How are you?" he asked her.

She looked a little more relaxed. "Not bad, and you?" she asked, as they continued to walk through the aisle.

"Glad to have bumped into you. You haven't gone to Corporal's."

"I'm very busy with work. I don't get to go out too often."

"What is it you do again?" he asked.

"Finance and banking, privately for specific companies."

"You do that from home, or do you work at an office somewhere?"

"Home and I travel a lot."

He nodded. "Nice." He looked at her cart.

"Feeding an army?" he asked.

"Company coming over tomorrow for lunch."

His chest tightened as he held her gaze, and she stopped. He covered her hand with his and looked down into her eyes. "Not another man or men, I hope," he said softly, but his tone was hard. He couldn't help it. He had a deep voice, and he never had to beg a woman for attention before. Most threw themselves at him. Another reason why he was interested in April. She eyed over his chest and then his lips.

"I had that handled back there."

"I didn't think so. Couldn't risk some other guys moving in on you. Not when my brothers and I want to get to know you better."

"Aqua," she said and turned away, but he slid his hand up her arm to her shoulder then reached up and cupped her cheek. He stroked her jaw, and so badly he wanted to press his lips to hers. April smelled incredible.

"What is it? You can't tell me that you aren't attracted to me. I can feel your heart beating as fast as mine is."

Her lips parted, and she went to speak and then hesitated. "I don't date. Not right now anyway. I'm so busy with work, and I have a few business trips coming up. It's not a good time for me."

"Who's coming over for lunch?" He stroked her jaw then slid his hand to her waist and stepped closer.

She inhaled. "None of your business." He squinted at her.

"So it's a date?"

"It's not your business. I'm sorry, Aqua, but I can't entertain you. I'm certain there are plenty of other women that would love to be the next adventure for you and your brothers. If you'll excuse me." She pulled away and began to walk.

"You have my things," he said to her, and she had to stop. When she did, he pressed up against her back, his lips against her ear and neck, and she didn't pull away or smack him. No, instead she tightened up and tilted to the left, giving him room to kiss her skin. He did and trailed his lips along her neck to her shoulder. "You wouldn't be an adventure. I hope to see you soon," he said and then stepped back and reached into her cart to grab his eggs and milk. She stared at him, and he saw and felt the attraction. She was resistant, and he couldn't help but to wonder why.

Chapter Three

"Wow, I didn't even know about this street, never mind this house back here. What did you say April does for a living?" Fogerty asked Amelia. Amelia was in awe of the place. The road was all private and led up a long sandy road appearing like it was heading nowhere, and then there were a set of security gates. Not too fancy, but definitely provided security. They opened before they reached the intercom.

"Something with finance and banking, I think. She travels often. That's why she isn't always around."

"Are those maids' quarters?" Dell asked, looking toward a large building that was a cross between a garage and a cottage. The view of the ocean appeared instantly and the sun shining along the house. It wasn't a huge mansion, but a pristine home, multiple floors and stunning. Amelia couldn't seem to focus on where to look next. It was gorgeous, and like something out of a magazine.

"She lives here alone?" Fogerty asked.

"As far as I know," Amelia said as Watson parked the truck. The front door opened, and April appeared, wearing capri pants in white and a pink sleeveless blouse. She looked sophisticated and classy.

They all got out, and April greeted them with a hug to Amelia and then kisses and hugs hello to the men.

"This place is gorgeous April," Amelia said to her.

"Thank you so much."

"I never even knew this road existed," Watson said, and April nodded.

"It's nice and private, and one of the reasons why I loved it when I came here about a year or so ago. Come on inside. I made some sweet tea, and I have beer, wine, whatever you would like."

"A tour," Amelia said and grinned. April took her arm and smiled. "So how was the first class?"

Amelia made a face. "Not good."

April released her arm as she showed them the open plan and entered the gorgeous kitchen. The view of the ocean as her back yard was breathtaking.

"North would go nuts over this place."

"I'm sure she would. So what happened?" April asked as she pointed to the beers and tea, and the guys picked out bottles of cold beer. Amelia went for the sweet tea with April.

"I can't do it. I was freaking out with the men in the class, the enclosed space, and then flashbacks of things. I'm not ready," Amelia repeated.

"What about one-on-one training in a more subdued setting?" April asked.

"We mentioned training her ourselves," Fogerty said and gave Amelia a sympathetic grin.

"I've been depending on you guys for everything," Amelia said and then looked away. "I don't want to talk about it. Let's look around. Give us a tour?" she asked April.

"Of course, and then lunch out on the patio if you all want to."

"Definitely with a view like that," Dell added and smiled.

* * * *

April could tell that the men were impressed with her place and Amelia, too. She had her stories straight about financing and banking, throwing in her success with the right investments. Which was completely true. Back in New York she backed her friend's son in a restaurant he wanted to open, and soon she was a silent partner and he opened a chain of them. From there she began to financially back different people for different things. It was lucrative, and she also knew that her real career would burn her out quickly emotionally and physically or a bullet even faster. She swallowed hard, and when they were done, they walked onto the patio with plates full of food.

The men didn't even question the two locked rooms she avoided showing them, saying that they were her work offices and space. There would be no way to explain all the high-tech equipment and computers, as well as her surveillance room that kept her abreast of anyone coming onto the property or even on the beach, which was private with multiple signs on either end.

"This is stunning, and the pool is gorgeous, too, with the waterfall and all that stone work," Dell complimented.

"We should do something like this at our place. Make it more relaxing and inviting when we entertain," Watson said while looking around at the view. "Is that your own entrance to the beach?" he asked, pointing down.

"Sure is."

"You ever worry about security, you know, living here alone and with such privacy?" Fogerty asked her.

"I have a high-tech security system. In fact, you guys would probably love it considering your line of work and all," she said, and they looked at her like she wasn't supposed to know they were mercenaries.

Then they looked at Amelia. "I didn't say a word," Amelia said.

April snickered. "She didn't tell me. It wasn't difficult to figure out that your specialties are beyond traditional military. You also were talking about the Quincy 5000 at Corporal's one night, and then add in a few details that slipped here and there and I figured mercenaries or something like that. Anyway, your secret is safe with me." She took a seat and then brought her glass of tea to her lips.

"How would you know about the Quincy 5000? That's not even public knowledge," Watson asked.

She gave a soft smile. "I have a few clients with connections, and two who are techies and get their hands on some awesome stuff. In fact, Mylo, a guy I know, was here a few months ago and set up the surround sound system as well as all the lighting and even the waterfalls and lights and, well, just about everything. I can do it all from my phone." She then pulled out her cell phone, hit the button, and some dance music came on all around the pool area and patio as well as inside.

"That is awesome," Amelia blurted.

"Look at this," she said and stood up and walked by Fogerty. "Step forward just a hair." When he did, she hit the button, and flames came up on the torches around the patio. "I can control everything from my phone or from the main pad on the wall right there in the kitchen or even from a remote. Mylo was here for a week. It was crazy."

"Mylo a boyfriend?" Dell asked, surprising her and apparently Amelia, as well.

"Dell," Amelia said as April turned everything off except the music and then sat down.

"I'm curious," he said and took a seat then a slug from his bottle of beer. Watson and Fogerty sat next to Amelia and could look at the view of the ocean and beach.

"He is just a friend."

"I bumped into Caden the other day. He said he saw you jogging down by the marina. That's like six or so miles from here at least," Watson said.

"I do that run several times a week. Different times of the day and sometimes at night. It depends on my mood and work schedule. It's fourteen miles in total." She took a forkful of chicken salad.

"Fourteen miles? Holy crap. I don't think I could run two miles," Amelia said. She looked at her.

"You have to build yourself up to doing it. I've been running for years. I do a lot of different activities to stay in shape. In fact, I kind of had an idea when you said you didn't feel comfortable at the Y doing those self-defense classes."

"What idea is that?" Amelia asked.

"I'll show you after we're done."

They talked about town and about the upcoming events as well as the boardwalk fair that was going on Sunday. There would even be fireworks in the evening on the beach.

"I think we're all going to go. Casey, North, Melina, Kai, and Afina, too."

"I think Ghost and Cosmo have a setup along the beach with stuff from Corporal's as well as the local police department. Caden is in charge of a special opening ceremony event honoring fallen soldiers and first responders," Dell told her.

"That's really nice. I'm certain Kai has things set for Guardians Hope as well?" she asked.

"Definitely, so you have to come, too," Amelia said.

"I'll see. I may be leaving for business next week, and I'm not sure of the details or when yet."

"Where to?" Dell asked her.

"That all depends on the client. More than likely north," she said, and then they started cleaning up from lunch.

She looked at Amelia who gave her shoulder a nudge. "Are you okay that they're here with me?" she asked.

April squinted at her. "Of course. Why wouldn't I be?"

Amelia glanced that way.

"I don't know. I mean, you're so independent and strong. I'm not feeling very strong at all," Amelia admitted and then swallowed hard. April felt badly for her, and she really wanted to help her friend gain back some confidence and also to feel like a new life began for her.

"You will get through this. Those three men adore you and are rocks for you. They'll stand by your side as you gain back that courage and confidence."

"Sometimes I feel like I disappoint them. That's why I pushed myself to go to that self-defense training and kickboxing class with Casey. She's only been going for a couple of weeks, and I can see a change in her already."

"Well, what was it that freaked you out or made you feel like you couldn't do it?"

"Well, there were strangers there, men and women, and glass on one side of the room where people walking by can watch. The instructors were nice, but I think it was too fast-paced. Like maybe I needed one on one, but my men wouldn't allow that, and I truly wouldn't be comfortable with a strange man I didn't know showing me things. I felt uneasy and panicked."

"Hmm, well, maybe you're going about this all wrong. Maybe you need to ease into things in a more relaxed setting. I want to show you something." She looked at the men who were standing by the pool and looking at the water. Dell was checking out one of the security cameras she had by the stairs leading toward the beach.

"Guys, do you mind if I show Amelia something? We'll be right at the building across from where you parked."

"Sure, we'll give you guys some time to talk," Watson said and gave Amelia a wink. Then Amelia and April headed through the kitchen and living room to the front door then out to the gym.

* * * *

"What do you think?" Dell asked Watson and Fogerty the second the front door closed.

Watson whistled. "Caden will not handle things well. He's already a mess."

"A mess? What do you mean?" Dell asked.

"Caden keeps trying to talk to April, even walked up to her at the pier, and she blew him off. He gets the feeling like she's hiding something."

"Same with Aqua and Simon, but if she even invites them here, they are going to go nuts over the tech stuff she is into. Obviously she's super smart. She ran through the controls like nothing, and these cameras are high-tech. I almost missed them," Dell added.

"Banking and finance can definitely put you in touch with some big shots. How long do you think it will be before Caden or his brothers dig deeper?" Watson asked.

"Not long at all. They've never had a woman on their radar before. April won't know what hit her once they go Navy Seal," Fogerty said, and Watson chuckled.

"I like her. I think she would be a good fit for them, but they won't like the whole traveling thing for business," Dell said.

"Or the guys who hook her up with tech stuff for her home," Watson added.

"Yeah, this should be interesting to see it go down. Do you think she'll go to the event Sunday?" Dell asked.

"Maybe, but Amelia mentioned everyone hanging out at Corporal's Friday night."

"Should be interesting to see what goes down," Watson said.

"I'm not too sure about that," Fogerty added, and they chuckled and looked at the view, giving Amelia and April some time to talk privately.

"She's a good friend to Amelia, and obviously Amelia feels comfortable talking with her. I wonder what she wanted to show Amelia," Dell said. One look at his brothers and he could tell they were curious, as well.

* * * *

"Oh my goodness, April, this is incredible," Amelia said, taking in the sight of the full gym and training center. April had every kind of machine, weights, an area of mats to spar, gloves, dummies, and so many things.

"I love to work out and train. It helps with stress and, well, prepares me in case someone was to try something. I know several forms and am always learning more."

"This is so impressive. How long have you been doing this kind of stuff?"

"For years. Pretty much since I was young. I was thinking that perhaps, if you are interested, you could come here and we could train together. I could introduce you to the basics, or we could do yoga to help relax you, and even traditional working out or whatever until you felt comfortable to try more."

The sound of the door opening alerted them to the guys coming in. April saw their eyes widen as they came into the building.

"Holy shit," Fogerty said, and April chuckled.

"This is some personal gym. You know how to use all this stuff?" Fogerty asked, immediately looking at the mats and the sparring equipment.

"Some might be for show," she lied and didn't make eye contact with him. She could tell that their minds were spinning, and they had questions. April knew she was taking a chance here, but Amelia was such a sweet woman and a good friend. April didn't have any family, so she felt compelled to help Amelia out any way she could.

"I was thinking that if Amelia wanted to come by here and work out with me a couple of times a week to get comfortable with training, then we could work it out."

"You know self-defense?" Watson asked, eying her over.

"I know multiple forms of martial arts, and dab in a bit of different things, but after speaking with Amelia, I was thinking that she needs to ease into things. You know, a more calming setting, and beginning with some simple relaxation techniques." She walked over to the wall and pressed a button. The one wall began to rise, exposing the glass and a perfect view of the beach and ocean.

"Oh God," Amelia said stepping closer.

April smiled. "Gator put this in for me. He owns a solar company in California. Watch this." She then pressed another button, and the glass slid to the left, opening up all the way to bring the outdoors in.

She took a deep breath and exhaled. "This is a great spot to begin every morning before working out or training." She looked at Amelia, who had tears in her eyes. April squinted with concern, but then Amelia hugged her arm and reached out for Fogerty to take her hand since he was closest. April locked gazes with a very stern and concerned-looking Fogerty, but then his eyes went to Amelia and she saw the love, the affection he had for her.

"What do you think, Fogerty?" Amelia asked him as Watson and Dell joined them.

April looked at the men. "One of you can hang out in the house or anywhere nearby you want to while she's here. We'll work out a schedule around my work and anything you and Amelia have going on. We can start slow." She smiled at Amelia.

"April, I don't know what to say. This is so unexpected, so amazing."

"I have this place, this home, and I'm alone. You're my friend, and I felt that you could maybe use such things, such a spot to help kickstart your new life. You're strong, you're beautiful, and you have three amazing, handsome, capable men who love you so much that I feel it. You deserve to be happy, and to not feel any pain anymore," she said to her, and Amelia had tears in her eyes. April didn't want to get emotional. She stepped away and crossed her arms in front of her chest. "Well, maybe pain from sore muscles after working out." She winked. Amelia laughed and so did the guys, but she saw their expressions and hoped they didn't push for more answers about her life.

"I want to do it," Amelia said.

"Awesome. We can start after my trip, unless you want to start tomorrow morning."

"Could we? Start tomorrow morning?" Amelia asked.

"Definitely."

April smiled, and then they planned the time and what they would start with. She felt great about this idea and hoped that Amelia would benefit in a positive way.

Chapter Four

"I want to be sure that we can take what was sent to us from our inside people and investigate properly. These people seem to be many steps ahead of us. Just as we think we have a connection, a link, it disappears or our informant does," Mike stated over the phone.

"Mike, we're set to get the intel needed with your okay. It's going to be tricky, but I do have three people I trust in Syria now and they have access to gather intel. If you can get the locations, then I'll get confirmation on what's being shipped to where and from where," Pierre told him.

"The problem is that we're not a hundred percent sure if this is taking place in Syria. You got the intel and information like I did. I need more on those businessmen, and then we can assign men to them and have them go in to gather more."

"Okay, she'll work on that, and we'll be in touch. Remember to not push too much. There are others working on things because of the men lost a year ago."

"I hear you. Wish they would be willing to work together, instead of holding out."

"Holding out because of our commanders and the decisions they made to pull everyone out immediately. It's not with any of us," Pierre said.

"Well, April did kind of piss them off a bit, so maybe they're still pissed at her," Mike said and chuckled.

"She saved lives, and her own. Those Seals would have died if she hadn't reacted like she did. The colonel knows that, and so does his team. I think their need to avenge their friends' murders are on their minds, plus there's still the connection to that bombing at the military base. It very well could have been the same group we're tracking down," Pierre added.

"They respect April, or maybe they just have the hots for her like every guy that meets her," Mike teased.

"I'd watch that with her tonight. She said you're going as friends."

"I know, and she is a great friend. I respect her and care about her. We're going to bring closure to the agents and the soldiers that were killed because of these men. No doubt in my mind."

"Okay, keep me posted, and enjoy the evening."

"Oh, I plan on it," he said, and Pierre chuckled.

"You don't have a chance with her. You know that, right?"

"You mean because of those Seals and the chief?"

"Exactly. She's denying it. I think they would be good for her and a relationship would bring some normalcy to her life."

"Not sure she could do it for the simple fact that I don't think she's done working for the agency, even after we get Rosen Armique."

"You're right. No way. I'll take care of things on this end, and get the men on the team ready. Talk to you over the weekend."

* * * *

Caden Farmer was all decked out in a black suit and black tie. He didn't do tuxedos unless necessary. He leaned against the bar set up in the main lounge area where a large crowd of people stood around talking and preparing for the event. There were numerous tables set up for donations as well as to buy tickets for hundreds of items being auctioned. He already declined several pushy women looking for some fun tonight, and he glanced at his watch, thinking he could stand another thirty minutes tops before he snuck out the side door and headed to Corporal's.

He took another sip from his bottle of Bud Light, and his eyes caught sight of the backside of one sexy blonde. Holy shit, she was exceptional from the back. The dark, slinky black dress hugged her hips and ass, and her entire back was exposed, appearing like the only thing holding up the sexy dress was the one thin string on her neck. Her hair was pulled up in some intricate style, and when she slightly turned, greeting a few men he didn't know but who were definitely eating her up with their eyes, he realized who it was. He saw the outline of her full, large breasts, and as she turned he felt his heart skip a beat. "April," he whispered.

Her arms were toned and defined, indicating she worked out. He knew that though, had seen her jogging several early mornings through town. He had wanted to follow her, make sure she safely got home, because men looked at her and it bothered him. Even now as he watched her, he could see the men licking their lips, and then Mike Waters, a special agent who had been part of the investigation with Cavanaugh, came up behind her. He slid his arm around her waist, and she turned, looked up, and the man smiled wide. He whispered to her, kissed her cheek, and she smiled and then laughed at whatever he said. Caden continued to watch her and then immediately saw another man and a woman, semi-attractive, not as gorgeous and eye-turning as April, approach them. Mike acted possessive of April, kept her close as it appeared he introduced the woman and the man. The woman had daggers in her eyes as she gave April the once over, and April smiled, then turned into Mike's arms, had her palm on his chest, and gave a sexy pose. From where Caden watched, he zeroed in on the high cut of the dress on her thigh along with the side profile of her breast again. The woman was a centerfold model and could even win a Miss Fitness contest with the definition like she had.

He had no idea she was seeing Mike. Could she really be seeing him? He couldn't help but wonder as a sour taste filled his mouth. He put the beer down and couldn't believe how damn jealous he felt. He and his brothers talked about her. About her saying she didn't date because of work and traveling. Then he bumped into Watson in town this morning after coming back from April's house. Watson told him how impressive the beach home was, and also how much April was doing for Amelia. It just added to her appeal and also made him have a thousand questions for her. Then he watched the woman and man walk away. Mike gave April a wink, and then they began to walk around the event. Caden watched, growing more and more jealous until he just couldn't stay away.

* * * *

"That was so awesome. Cynthia looked shocked, and her boyfriend, holy shit, he actually licked his lips looking at you. Which, by the way, you are so hot. I swear I wish you would consider the friends with benefits thing." He stroked her back.

"You're an idiot. We talked about this." She looked at her watch. "An hour then I'm out, unless your pouty ex-girlfriend makes her boyfriend leave. What did you say he does for a living?"

"Real estate tycoon."

"You mean you didn't check him out?"

"What do you think?" he asked and made a funny face like she was silly for asking that question.

She chuckled. "You like her that much?"

"I thought I did. I think maybe I was just worrying about the time it took to actually date her, from a relationship between work and the heavy caseload. Maybe I just wanted to hold on to her out of convenience. You know, it would be easier than starting over." He took a sip from his beer.

"I get that, but eventually it would have ended. Your job requires a lot of hours day and night, and being called out at any time. A lot of women can't handle that."

"Just like a lot of men can't," he said and winked. She nodded.

"Oh boy, here comes those three guys with ATF that are hot for you," Mike said just as another man approached him, and he turned away.

"Miss Marris, so good to see you again." She turned to look up to see Dom and his two buddies, Lou and Frank. She met them a couple of weeks back at Murphy's pub and restaurant, and Mike introduced her. At first she thought they were kind of interesting, but she didn't really feel an attraction. She felt the hand on her hip as Dom leaned down to kiss her cheek hello. She was polite and the same with Lou and Frank as they kissed her hello.

"You look amazing. Please tell me Mike isn't your date," he said.

"He is my date. How about you guys? How is everything going?" she asked and took a sip from her glass of champagne.

"It's going well, but would be better if you were our date. How about you break away from him and come along with us to check out the views on the balcony?" Frank asked, eyeing her over. She chuckled.

"Not going to happen, but nice try. Hey, I thought you hooked up with that cute little redhead that night at Murphy's. What happened with her? She seemed really into you guys."

They looked shocked that she knew. She watched people and saw things most didn't.

"Nothing happened. Except fulfilling her fantasies," Lou said and licked his lower lip and gave her a wink.

She laughed, and then Mike turned around. "Hey, guys, what's up? Thanks for keeping my date company. You ready, baby?" Mike asked and slid his arm around her waist.

"Later, guys, enjoy the evening," she said and could see their angry and disappointed faces.

"I'm making enemies with you as my date. I have to work with those boneheads, you know."

She chuckled. "I'm making enemies with you as my date, as well," she said, looking around as they walked. She nearly stumbled when she caught sight of Caden Farmer. Holy shit, he looked incredible. She quickly turned away, and then Mike was greeted by someone else.

"Excuse me a minute. We'll catch up later. I need to use the ladies' room," she told him.

He nodded and then continued talking, but he watched her head toward the hallway and ladies' room, the opposite direction she saw Caden. Jesus, he looked pissed off and ready to kill someone. She found the ladies' room, and then after she was finished, she walked out to see the outdoor patio doors to the right. She could use the breather. She wanted to waste a little time and then head out.

She placed the champagne glass down on the high table and then looked out at the water and marina. It was a really nice venue, and there were so many people in attendance. She was glad for the fundraiser's success. As she took a deep breath of fresh air, she sensed someone come outside. A glance over her shoulder and she saw it was Caden. She turned. "Caden, how are you?" she asked. He didn't smile, just looked her over and then was in her space. He slid his arm around her waist.

"So good to see you, April." He leaned down to kiss her cheek hello. She turned slightly, and that soft peck did so much to her insides she felt nervous. Then he was pulling her closer, sliding his palm along her open back, and she gripped onto his forearms, tilting her head up toward him. The man was gorgeous, lethal, intense right now, and he felt and smelled so good.

"You look amazing. I didn't know you would be here."

"I came with Mike." She felt his hand stop stroking her skin along her back.

"I saw that. What's it all about? I thought you didn't date," he said, staring at her lips. She felt his palm over her lower back, partially over her ass. His finger stroked her there, instantly sending her body up in flames. Her lips parted in a low gasp.

She went to put some space between them, but he stepped closer, her rear hitting the railing.

"I..." She went to look away.

"Don't lie to me. I hate liars."

She looked back up into his eyes.

"I don't date, Chief. Mike and I are friends."

"Friends don't put their hands on your ass and act possessive."

"His hand never touched my ass," she said in a snappy tone.

He stared at her with such emotion she felt compelled to tell him the truth, but then he spoke and she stirred in his arms. "Fuck, I'm so fucking jealous it's eating me alive. Tell me you aren't fucking him. Tell me," he demanded, his hold so possessive. She could hardly breathe. He was incredibly sexy, so intense, and she shook her head and that was it. Caden moved in for the kill and kissed her, sliding his hand up her back to her neck, making that kiss erotic and wild. She pressed closer, kissed him back, and couldn't believe how turned on she was. Her mind went into fast forward. She wanted him. Wanted to feel his body close to hers. Wanted to inhale his scent and see what kind of a lover the chief of police was. Then she thought about Aqua and Simon and realized that if she allowed this, then they would be included. That freaked her out. That meant deep feelings, and it wouldn't be just sex. Did she want it to be more?

She started pulling back, but Caden wasn't ready to stop kissing her. His other hand went around her waist tight, making her lose her breath. When he finally released her lips, he trailed his mouth along her neck and into her top. She gripped him. "Caden, slow down. Jesus, we need to stop."

He looked up, appearing like some wild man, and she knew he was a Navy Seal. Knew his capabilities and his brothers', too. She thought of the moment they appeared in the hallway after she took Vince Turbin, that terrorist piece of shit, out. This was too complicated. The case was active, and she was pretty much smack in the middle.

He continued to hold her, let the hand that was on the back of her neck lower to her mid-back. His finger traced down her spine and along her sensitive skin. He stared down into her eyes as she caught her breath.

"Leave with me now. Come home with me, and let's stop this bullshit and explore this attraction." She licked her lips and pressed away from him. He released her but not completely.

She fixed her lips, felt how swollen and needy they were. She loved how demanding he was as he kissed her. How sexy and macho he held her and took control. She could get lost in that, but she needed to be smart. This wasn't smart at all.

"I won't do that."

"Why the hell not?" he asked, taking her hand and bringing it up against his chest. His other hand was on her waist. She swallowed hard.

"I don't know you, Caden. I don't sleep around."

"You let men take you to events and show you off as their trophy, though. What does he have on you to make you come here as his date?"

She squinted at him and his untrusting, accusatory comment.

"No one forces me to do anything." She went to pull away, and he snagged her back and kissed her again. This was insane, and as they dueled for control of the kiss, he squeezed her ass, pulled her so tight she felt his thick, hard erection and moaned into his mouth. His other hand cupped her breast and stroked her nipple. Her pussy clenched, and she felt the cream drip. Son of a bitch, he was a piece of work. No man affected her like Caden.

When he finally released her lips, he pulled her against his chest and hugged her to him. "Come home with me now. I'll call Aqua and Simon." She thought about it a moment but then remembered that everyone expected to see her at Corporal's and she still needed to play the role as Mike's date tonight. She pulled back. "Don't," he said through clenched teeth. Was she making him this crazy? Was he really so jealous over Mike and other men wanting her?

"I have to stay a little longer. Mike needs me."

"Needs you?" he asked in anger.

"To be his date. He's trying to piss off an ex-girlfriend."

"What?" he asked, seeming shocked.

"I know, I know, very sophomoric, but she broke his heart and left him for another man. So far it's working."

"The brunette that was throwing spears at you with the older guy who was totally licking his lips watching you?" he asked, sliding his palm along her ass. She nodded.

"I want to be alone with you. So do Aqua and Simon."

"I have to go to Corporal's, Caden, and I don't think I'm ready for some public display of barbaric possession or claim of sorts. I don't want that. I have a lot going on in my life, in business, and I—"

He kissed her again until she was breathless. When he pulled from her mouth, she exhaled. "Stop doing that."

"Can't help it. Everything about you is sexy and gets me fired up. I want you. Want to explore every inch of you with my brothers, and I don't want the excuses."

"I don't think I can give you what you're asking for, Caden."

"Why not?" he asked.

"It's complicated."

"What isn't? You feel the attraction to the three of us. You want no strings, then no fucking strings."

She thought about that. Is that what she wanted? She could tell it wouldn't go that way. They would all want more, and perhaps it would get serious fast and then she would have to lie to them and lie some more. She felt like shit.

"What's wrong? What is it? Talk to me."

"To be honest, I'm confused. I have trust issues. I really don't date."

"But you're attracted to us. You want to explore these feelings?"

She nodded her head.

"Then let's plan on doing that tonight. We leave here, meet casually at the bar, and hang with friends, and then we leave."

"Not together. I don't want this turning into something it can't be." She saw his insulted expression, and she gripped his hips. "Caden, trust issues. Some past damage from previous relationships, and my lifestyle, my work schedule, and the fact that making any kind of commitment isn't possible."

He seemed to think about that.

"One day at a time. No complications," he said, and she stared at him. He stroked along the side of her breast then to her back again. She loved the way it felt.

"One day at a time," he said, and she nodded. As she went to pull away, he shook his head. "One last taste to hold me off until later." He pressed his lips to hers. This kiss was slow, deep, and meaningful, unlike the full-throttle shock and awe of his first assault on her lips and her defenses. It felt so good, and it felt incredibly right.

* * * *

"Where is he now?" Kulta asked. He worked for Victoria and had men keeping tabs on Agent Mike Waters.

"He's with the blonde," the guy told him over the phone, and then Kulta heard his phone go off, indicating another text message. Kulta was sending pictures. He glanced at it and whistled.

"She is exceptional. Wonder what she sees in this agent," the guy said.

"Keep watch. I'll be in touch if they want anything done tonight."

"Understood."

Kulta ended the call and looked at the pictures. He was right, the woman was exceptional. He heard the door open to the office and gave Victoria a nod. "They have their eyes on the agent and the woman he's with."

"Another agent?"

"No, a date." He passed his phone to her to see. She widened her eyes.

"Who is she?"

"We don't know yet, but I have men working on it." She stared at her and zoomed in. The guy got good shots of the woman.

"I want to know more." She looked like she was up to something.

"What color are her eyes?" she asked and then licked her lips and tapped her chin. He squinted.

"Seriously, Victoria?"

"I owe Rosen, and he has a good friend, a powerful one who has unique tastes. He'll be with Rosen in a couple of weeks. Get me what you can on her, and I mean everything."

Kulta nodded, and she handed him back his phone but not before she forwarded the pictures to herself.

* * * *

"Is it me or am I getting daggers thrown at me from Caden, Simon, and Aqua?" Mike asked her, whispering into her ear as he stood next to her at the bar. His two buddies from the state police were there, too. She knew who they were, but they hadn't a clue as to who she was. No one here did, and she was fine keeping it that way. She reached up and rubbed her temple.

"Are you feeling okay? I can drive you home now," he said and took a sip from his beer.

"You don't need to leave because of me. Besides, I think that little redhead talking to Phillip wants to talk to you again," she said, and he looked toward where the redhead was.

"You don't mind?"

"Mike, everything worked out well tonight. Enjoy. I'm going to go visit with my friends," she said, and he nodded and then gave her a hug and kissed her cheek by her ear.

"Be sure about those Navy Seals, okay," he said, and she nodded.

He walked away, and she stepped from the bar only to be stopped by Ice as she was passing by. He looked her over and smiled. "You look incredible. Heard you helped Mike out with an ex-girlfriend," he said, and she chuckled.

"He tell you that?" she asked.

"Sure did. I also heard about your plan with Amelia. I think it's great, and she seems thrilled with the idea."

"Wow, seems word travels fast around here. I should be careful."

"Word travels fast when someone is a good person and people care. I'm curious to know where you learned martial arts and relaxation techniques like what Amelia explained to me."

"She told you about it?"

"She was thrilled, although I didn't think a lot of civilians, well, people with no military backgrounds knew about it."

She was prepared for this and was on her toes. "Yeah, well, I learned at a young age. My dad was a Marine and a cop. I heard about the techniques and saw him practicing several times before his shifts for work or during training in the gym. I was enthralled with it and started to investigate further. When he saw I was interested so much, he taught me, as well."

She felt the hand on her hip and turned to the right and locked gazes with Simon. "Is the date with Mike finally over?" he asked, and Ice chuckled.

"Why do you want to know?" she asked with a little bit of attitude.

His hand firmed on her hip and then slid along her waist as he kissed her bare shoulder. "So my brothers and I could snag your full attention now."

She looked at Ice, who squinted but was smirking. "Well, Ice and I are actually talking."

"Join us, Simon," Ice said, and the bartender gave Simon a nod and then handed him a cold beer.

She couldn't help but to feel aroused by Simon this close to her. The man was filled with muscles, his shoulder and neck muscles were bulging, and the gruff along his cheeks and chin made him appear wild and rugged, yet his skin looked soft, tanned, and he was definitely a looker. He smelled really good, too, and as he joined them, he pulled her between his legs as he stood by the bar and she faced Ice.

"So you were saying that your dad was a Marine and a cop. What else did he teach you?" Ice asked.

"A lot of things," she said, and then Aqua and Caden appeared. They said hello to Ice, and Casey and Melena came by, and the crowd around them grew a little bigger. She got off the interrogation a little but then was almost wishing for Ice to ask her more questions as Caden, Aqua, and Simon kept her close and took every opportunity to touch her.

She stepped to the side to say something to Casey, who was talking to Dion, an instructor at the Y. One look at Ice and April could tell he was jealous. She wondered if Ice would make a move on Casey and if his brothers would show up here, too. She felt the caress to her hip, and as she stepped back, Aqua pulled her into his arms. He stared down into her eyes and looked over the deep cleavage where her dress dipped. His fingers stroked her bare skin on her back, and she felt Caden and Simon press closer to her, as well.

"This dress is something else. Did Mike's plan work? Did his ex get jealous?" he asked, but it was as if Aqua was making sure there really wasn't anything romantic between her and Mike.

"Not sure. They kind of disappeared not long after Mike introduced me," she replied. Aqua held her gaze, and she held his. She stared at his dark blue eyes, that chiseled face filled with muscles. He was trim, completely in shape with not an ounce of fat on him. He looked military, hard and commanding. He wasn't as bulky and thick with muscles like his brothers were. He had more of a martial artist type of physique. His fingers were doing a number on her body, making her skin tingle and her pussy clench.

"Are you ready to go home? We want to be alone with you," he said, and she worried about making a scene, about indicating she was leaving with them. They already grabbed everyone's attention.

She glanced at Caden. "I thought we discussed this."

"Come back to our place. Have a drink. We'll talk some more. They'll hang out a little longer and then meet us," he said, having it all planned out.

Aqua stroked her skin up and down her back all the way to where the material ended and her ass began. "Go with him now, April," he whispered, but she felt like it was an order. For some strange reason she was aroused by that, but she was always a little stubborn when it came to men.

"Nice try, Seal," she said and turned from his arms to reach for her drink that was on the bar. Her back was toward them, and she knew the dress was sexy, that it showed off her curves, her muscular back, and her tan with no tan lines. It was one of the many benefits of owning her own beach front property in a secluded piece of six acres. She took a sip from her drink then looked over her shoulder at them. They were in a dead stare. Caden had one hand in his pocket and the other held a beer bottle. Simon sat next to Aqua on the two stools right next to her, blocking anyone from invading this little gathering. "So tell me, Caden, what made you retire from the Seals and become the chief of police of Mercy?"

He stepped closer, holding her gaze and making her feel like no one else mattered, nothing else mattered but talking to her and focusing on her. She shifted her body to turn toward him.

"Was time for a change. My father and grandfather were in law enforcement around here. I came back right before he was getting ready to retire with his brothers and our mom, and the people voted me in." Her eyes widened. She stood up straighter.

"Did you say your father, his brothers, and your mom?" He nodded.

Simon stepped to her right side and stroked her elbow. She glanced way up at him, and he brought her hand to his lips and kissed her knuckles.

"The tradition is strong in our family, April," he said and lowered her hand to his thigh, still holding it.

Her mind was a whirlwind of thoughts. These men could be looking for their perfect woman, the one who would be at their beck and call and be a wife, and maybe even bear their children. She gulped.

"Does that scare you? A ménage?" Aqua said, reaching out on her left side to gently rub his thumb along her bare neck as he stared down at her. They surrounded April like a blanket of safety, security, and she couldn't believe how her body vibrated from them being so close.

"I know people who are involved in them. Knew of ménage relationships back in New York," she said, trying to act unaffected, hoping they weren't hinting that she could be the one for them, then hoping that if miracles happened she could be.

Then she thought about the lies she told, and the others she had yet to tell. Like the ones about the bullet wounds and where they really came from. Surely if they ever found out the truth, then they would realize that she had no choice. It was a mission, a situation gone all wrong, and she should actually be dead.

She felt the fingertips under her chin and saw Caden right in front of her. "Hey, you okay? We lost you there a moment."

She gave a nod. "I'm fine. So you decided to follow the family footsteps?" she asked, thankfully remembering what exactly they were talking about.

"I did, and been here for three years now."

"What about you two? Any thoughts to retiring and joining the force since you have a great connection?" she asked them.

"No," Aqua said very quickly.

"Not for me," Simon said and took her glass from her hand and placed it onto the bar behind her.

Caden put his hands on her hips. He stroked her hip bones. "What about you? What kind of work do you do, and how often do you have to travel?" he asked.

"I'm into finance and banking. I have to travel often. Lots of spur of the moment trips." Caden leaned closer. She stared at his lips.

"We're wasting precious time. I want every moment with you tonight." He pressed his lips to hers. It was soft, quick, like a tease, and it worked. She held his gaze as Simon and Aqua continued to caress her skin. Three of them teaming up on her was not fair at all.

A loud eruption of laughter brought her out of her daze and back to the present. She lowered her eyes and looked away.

"Let's go," Caden said and took her elbow. She looked at Simon and Aqua, who turned around to face the bar and got two more beers.

Caden slid his arm around her waist and guided her from the bar. No one even seemed to notice them leaving, and she didn't even care. He brought her out the side entrance and to his truck. He hit unlock, but before he opened the door he pulled her toward him, kissed her as he pressed her back to the door. She kissed him back, ran her fingers through his hair, and held on to him. His large, warm, capable hand squeezed her ass. When he released her lips he looked so wild. He was breathing through his nostrils. "No games, April. No holding back. Tonight. We got tonight." He stepped back and opened the door. She went to get in, but he lifted her up and placed her onto the seat.

"Oh." She gasped.

"Just wait," he said and then closed the door. The anticipation was wild, and she couldn't ever remember feeling so high strung, so in need of sex. These men did it to her. As he started the truck and pulled out of the parking lot, she looked over her shoulder, wondering if Aqua and Simon were leaving, too.

"One beer, maybe, and then they'll head home. That means I'm in charge of getting you ready for the three of us," he said to her. He reached over and caressed her inner thigh. He pulled her slightly, letting her know he wanted her to scoot over. He was definitely a commanding, demanding man. She slid right over and undid the button on his dress shirt then slid her palm right in. He was hard, warm, and so was his hand that pressed between her legs.

"I don't think going slow will be possible, April. The sight of you in this dress tonight, and all the men wanting what is going to be mine and my brothers, really tried my patience," he said, his voice hard, thick, and filled with promises.

She pulled her hand from his shirt and then leaned in to kiss his neck as he drove. Then she placed her hand over his dress pants and cock. He was huge, thick, and hard.

"Sweet Jesus, woman, I'm so fucking close. You drive me wild."

"I feel it, too. It's insane, and I would never just head home with three men I hardly know at all."

"We're going to get to know one another really well tonight."

She pressed her lips to his neck and sucked on a sensitive spot. His forearm tightened along with his hold on the steering wheel.

"Remember what I said, Caden. This timing is so bad for me. I have a lot of business coming up, trips and things."

His grip on her inner thigh tightened. "We'll work it out," he said and then stepped on the gas, made a sharp turn, and headed down a long road with very few houses on it. When he pulled onto another road and then along the water near the marina, she realized he had his own nice-sized piece of property and an older home. There were no neighbors. It was private and very, very dark out. He put the truck in park and turned off the ignition. She went to slide away, and he pulled her back, turned slightly, and lifted her to her knees. He kissed her as he ran his hands over her skin and her back. When he released her lips, he started giving orders.

"Come on," he said and then opened his door and helped her out. He lifted her against his chest and slowly let her slide down his body.

They walked to the door when she heard another truck speeding along the road. He chuckled. "You got us all in a state, woman," he said, and she felt a little giddy about that. She was one woman about to have sex with three men. As they got into the house, he turned on the light, and she looked around the place, impressed with the cleanliness and how neat the kitchen counter was. Then suddenly Caden lifted her up against him and started kissing her again. She ran her fingers through his hair, then started to undo his tie and shirt when she felt his palm slide up her dress. He lifted her up, her ass landed on the cold, hard granite, and she gasped at the contrast to the heat running through her veins. They were both wild with need, unable to get enough, to feel enough. He pulled from her mouth and yanked down her panties, and she shoved open his dress shirt, ran her palms up and down his chest as he undid the button to his pants.

"Protection? Do I need anything?" he asked.

"No. Oh God, I have an IUD," she said, and he undid his pants the rest of the way, stepped from his shoes, shoved his pants down, and then found her pussy and slid two fingers into her cunt as he held her gaze. The intensity of their locked gazes had her moaning and her pussy wet. She gasped when another finger slid over her asshole. She tilted back as she heard the door slam closed behind Simon.

"Fuck," Aqua said, and he and Simon started pulling off their shirts, looking at her with such hunger she came.

"Sweet. Holy fuck, I want to see her naked. I want to kiss and suck every inch of her," Aqua demanded. Their tones were so fierce. She felt almost intimidated, but the arousal was much stronger.

"Can't wait. We got all night. I can't fucking wait," Caden said, slowly moving his fingers from her cunt and then lowering his mouth to her pussy. He licked and sucked, and she moaned and tilted her pelvis toward him. He spread her legs wide, her dress to her hips, his palms sliding under her ass to pull her over the edge. She felt his hot, wet tongue lash out at her cunt then glide over her asshole back and forth.

"Caden." She grunted and reached for his head and rocked her hips.

When he lifted up, his lips glistened, the veins by his temples pulsated, and he looked carnal. "Mine. Now," he ordered.

She shivered and held his gaze. "Yes. Yes, Caden, I need you now." He pulled her a little more forward, and the tip of his cock hit her oversensitive pussy lips, making her moan as he yanked her toward him, his cock infiltrating her pussy in one fast stroke.

"Oh!" they both moaned, then held on to one another a moment.

She was breathing heavily. "Caden."

"I know. I fucking know," he said, and that was it. He started to thrust into her pussy, was basically taking her against the kitchen island for the first time, and she didn't even care. She gripped onto his shoulders and counter thrust.

"It's been so long," she admitted. "Oh God, you feel so good. So hard. More, Caden. More," she cheered.

She looked at his chest, could see all the scars and then the gunshot wounds. One, two, three, four. She reached out, and he grabbed her hand. "No. Not now. Just let go and be with me," he demanded. She felt the tears reach her eyes. She knew in that moment there was more to this than just sex. He had been shot like she had. She knew it was coming. That they would see and question her. There was no turning back.

"Son of a bitch," Simon said, and he pressed closer, gripped her cheeks, and kissed her hard on the mouth, pulling all thoughts but his lips and his demanding hold to the front of her focus. He slowly lowered her body as Caden continued to thrust his thick, hard cock into her cunt.

"Oh, Caden. Oh please. Please," she cried out.

"So incredible. You're incredible. I'm there, baby," he said, and Simon slid the straps of her dress down, exposing her full, round breasts.

"Gorgeous," Aqua said, joining them on the other side.

"April. April!" Caden said and came inside of her. She lifted her top as he held on to her, and then her eyes locked onto Simon's. He looked shocked.

"April?" he questioned, and she knew he saw the first scar from the bullet wound. She licked her lower lip and reached out to him. He took her hand and brought it against his cheek.

"What's wrong?" Caden asked and looked from Aqua to Simon and then to April.

She lifted up with Caden's help. His cock slid from her pussy, making her feel the loss, the depth of the emotions she experienced having sex with Caden. She swallowed hard so she could deal with the present situation and released Simon's cheek.

He caressed her shoulder, gave it a reassuring squeeze before he pressed her top lower, stroking over her breast and the scar.

"Is it a bullet wound?" Simon asked.

"What?" Caden asked and looked down. He squinted, and Aqua was right there, too, looking completely pissed off.

"Yes, it is. It happened a while ago. I have two. The other right above my rib."

"Holy shit, how?" Caden asked.

"Drive-by shooting. I was in high school, senior year. I should have died," she said, the lie already off her lips, having practiced it thousands of times. Never once did it accompany the guilty feeling she had right now lying to them.

"Holy shit," Caden said and pulled her into his arms and hugged her, shocking her. She squeezed him tight, then felt Aqua and Simon's hands on her back, caressing her, too.

She pulled back and looked at their chests of muscles, of scars they sported, and reached out, but Caden grabbed her hips as Aqua gave an order.

"The bedroom, so we can lay her out and take our time learning every inch of her," Aqua said.

* * * *

Caden could see it in her eyes. She lied. He didn't know why or for what reason, and he hoped it wasn't something bad, like people were after her and she was in hiding or something. He just didn't know, and his gut clenched. This wasn't good at all. He was conflicted. She was shot like he was. She survived like he did. She could understand. He felt overwhelmed.

Slowly he set her feet down, and they began to slide her dress from her body. With every inch of skin, his hunger began to increase. He couldn't believe he didn't even get her into the bedroom and basically attacked her and fucked her on the kitchen island. He felt a bit embarrassed, and the thought of expressing it to April and showing vulnerability pissed him off, so he acted macho instead.

He lifted her up into his arms and carried her to the bedroom. Her feminine arms wrapped around his shoulders, and she kissed his neck, his bare shoulder. "Next time, we go slow. I didn't mean to attack you like that," he whispered.

"Caden." She said his name as he held her in his arms right in front of the bed. "I loved it. I wanted it, too. It was perfect," she said, easing his mind. He winked.

"Next time, slow." He pressed his lips to hers. He slowly set her feet down, her dress completely off, slid to the floor. He took a sharp breath at the sight of her. Perfection. There she stood in her heels and nothing else.

He stepped back as Aqua and Simon began to explore her body, starting with the other scar right above her ribs on the left side. She was muscular with dips and ridges, a woman who was in excellent physical condition. Even her ass was exquisite. He was getting aroused all over again, watching Aqua's hand slide over her ass and then his lips beginning to feast on her very large breasts.

"You're the most beautiful, sexiest woman I've ever laid eyes on, and that's no bullshit, April," Simon told her and lowered his mouth to kiss the scar above her left breast. She closed her eyes, and his brothers began to prepare her for them next.

* * * *

Aqua was shocked and couldn't help the uneasy feeling he had. Was he so distrusting that he thought when April said she nearly died in a drive-by shooting that she lied, or did she? Why would she lie? Was she in trouble, or had been at one time? She was so private, and didn't share much about her life or her past. He didn't want to focus on that. His body definitely didn't want to focus on anything but making her his, sharing her with his brothers, and claiming her their woman. This was not just about sex and feeling lust. He was jealous all night knowing men stared at her, wanting her, and that she went to that fundraiser with Mike.

He suckled her nipple a little harder. She moaned and tightened. "Aqua." She said his name. Then Simon cupped her cheek, and they lowered her to the bed.

"Spread your legs. Offer us this pussy," Aqua commanded, his mind on claiming her and marking her in every way so she would never want another man but him and his brothers. He eased his palm along her thighs and stroked a finger along her groin. She tightened and reached down toward his hand.

"No. Keep them above your head. Show us how much you want us next," Simon told her and eased her one hand up above her. She moved the other one and then held Aqua's gaze as she widened her thighs and lifted her torso. He winked at her, her nipples hardened on her breasts, and Simon lowered down to kiss her on the mouth as Aqua lowered down to lick up and into her cunt.

He swirled his tongue over her cream. Her taste fed his desires.

"So delicious. You're wet for us, baby, and I got something for you right here." He tapped his cock against her pussy, and she moaned.

"Don't tease me, Aqua. I've never done anything like this before, and I feel ready to snap. Please," she begged.

Simon cupped her jaw. "Never have sex with more than one man at once?" he asked. She shook her head.

"Good," Aqua and Caden said at the same time. She tilted her head back and moaned as Aqua began to push the tip of his cock into her pussy.

"Here I come, April. You're incredible. So fucking incredible," he said, and Simon released her jaw and then stepped to the side as Aqua began to thrust into her pussy, filling her with his cock. He held himself inside of her, and they both moaned.

"Jesus," he exclaimed. He felt so much. He felt emotional, a connection like nothing ever before. It was like he found the right fit, the perfect match to him, to his body and his soul. He was shocked at his thoughts, and he denied them and just thought about fucking her, claiming her. This was too much. He felt too much. What the fuck?

He gripped her hips and began to thrust faster and faster. She went to move her arms, and he slid his palms up her arms, to her wrists, and held them above her head while he thrust and stroked deeper, faster, his need for control overpowering everything else. He had a deep itch, and with every stroke it seemed to ease somehow. She was his. She belonged to them, and by the time they were done she would never have another man kiss her, suck on her breasts, make love to her, and be able to say she was his. No. She was theirs. "Mine. You're mine," he said and ground his pelvis deeper and deeper. She moaned, and then he felt her come. He couldn't hold back. The warmth, the lubrication did something to his cock.

"I'm there already. I'm fucking there already." He tried holding back, but with every stroke he felt himself losing control until he came inside of her. He exhaled and lay over her, caressed her cheeks, and pecked at her lips. "God I love your eyes, and this body, it's exceptional."

"You're not so bad yourself, Seal," she teased, and he chuckled, kissed her lips, and then eased up. "Simon needs you, too."

"I need Simon," she replied, and as Aqua eased out, Simon lifted her up and rolled over so she was straddling his waist. Her long blonde hair was falling from the updo she had. She reached up, her breasts sticking out, her hips and ass looking so hot. She was a sex symbol.

She started to pull out the pins in her hair as Simon stroked her ribs and her breasts.

* * * *

Simon caressed her skin as he watched April fix her hair. The updo from earlier was now a complete mess, but she looked sexy, wild, like his brothers made her crazy with need. Her warm, damp cunt sat right above his cock, and he wanted in. He stroked her breasts and looked at her nipples, perky and hard, then at the two scars. Bullet wounds. What the fuck?

He caressed one with the pad of his thumb and then eased up to stroke her nipples.

Her long blonde hair began to fall, and she shook her head and then ran her fingers through her hair. She looked even sexier. He gripped her hair and head and brought her down to kiss him. Their lips touched, and it was like fire, heat, need that overtook his body. He plunged his tongue into her deeply and then felt her jerk and moan.

"Such a sexy ass. Simon needs that pussy, baby. Ease on over him while I do a little exploring of my own," Caden said.

She moaned again and then eased up, pulling slowly from Simon's lips.

He licked his lower lip. "Come on and ride me," he said, and she lifted up and then jerked forward.

"Caden."

"Yeah, so tight but wet. Your asshole is sucking in my finger," he said, and she started to rock her hips.

"I never… Caden. Oh God, this is bad."

"Not bad. You never had a cock in your ass. Tonight we'll be everywhere, filling you up and claiming you ours," Aqua said and ran his palm under her hair, gripped her, and then pressed his mouth to hers. She lifted up, and Simon aligned his cock with her pussy and it was on. She lowered down and began to ride him as Caden thrust a finger into her asshole.

"I'll grab the lube after I wash up, and, Caden, you get that ass ready. I get her mouth."

Simon gripped her hips and thrust upward. "April, holy shit. April, you feel tight and hot. This is going to be incredible," he told her, and she moaned and rocked her hips and ass back.

Caden gripped her shoulder from behind her.

"Nice and easy. You feel it, April. Being in a ménage we claim all holes ours. Every inch of you will be ours, and we're all yours, too."

She moaned again. "I can't believe this. I need, Caden. Oh God, I can't believe I'm doing this. I feel so much," she admitted, and Simon smiled.

"It's perfect. You were made for us," he said and reached up to pull her down for a kiss. She moaned deeper. Apparently she felt Caden's finger strokes even more. She pulled from Simon's mouth.

"Caden."

"Just pulled out to get some lube. We're big men. We don't want to hurt you, not ever." He kissed her bare shoulder. She was panting now, and looking a little worried.

Simon cupped her cheek. "Easy, this will be incredible. You'll feel even more than you do right now."

"I don't know if I can handle more, Simon."

He chuckled. "You can handle all of us."

"Yes, she can," Aqua said and cupped her cheek and brought her head lower. Simon watched as she opened her mouth, and Aqua's thick, hard cock began to move in and out of her mouth.

She moaned again.

"Just a little lube, then we take you together." Simon thrust upward as Aqua slid in and out of her mouth. A moment later Simon moaned as Caden began to replace fingers with his cock. It was overwhelming. The connection, the sensations he felt rocked him as he thrust upward and Caden thrust into her ass.

"Holy fuck. Holy shit, baby, so good. So fucking good," he said, and then she moaned and Aqua grunted as the four of them made love together, thrusting, moaning, and instantly changing his ideas that he could never commit to a woman and that no one would be special enough to win his heart. Apparently there was something about April that affected him like nothing else ever had.

"I'm there. This mouth, woman. You're a goddess," Aqua said and pumped a few more times then came in her mouth. The moment he pulled out, April was gasping for breath.

"Oh, Caden, Simon. Oh please, I'm coming. I feel it." She started counter rocking against their cocks, and then she cried out her release as Simon came and then Caden followed. She collapsed against Simon's chest, and he kissed her neck, her shoulder as he held her tight.

"Incredible," Caden said, kissing her neck and her back and easing out of her ass.

Simon could feel him, and then he rolled her to her back, his cock limp and more than satisfied, as Simon looked at April and smiled. "You okay?" he asked, stroking her cheek.

"More than okay. That was amazing."

Aqua leaned against her back and slid his palm along her hip to her breast, cupping it. "We Seals aim to please," he said and kissed her. She giggled.

* * * *

April closed her eyes and exhaled. She couldn't believe that she just had sex with three men, and anal sex no less. She hadn't been with them for an hour, and here she was wanting more, analyzing her emotions and how connected she felt. This was dangerous. She had secrets, even ones that she knew if they knew about them they would understand. They were military, and they were Seals. Hell, the one guy she started seeing two years ago was a Seal. It was over before it got started because of their jobs, and he was killed while aiding in the rescue of her and the other agents. She hadn't found out until later, and she was so upset about everything, so affected by the case that she took a leave of absence. Now here she was in the middle of things again. Maybe in a safer spot, doing her work on computers and meeting up with Pierre wherever he asked her to be, but she was involved and couldn't let on to who she was. That was another thing. They were Seals, just like Evan. Not that she slept with Evan. Well, they came pretty close, but the jobs got in the way. They were friends, and then disaster struck. She looked at Aqua. His eyes held hers as she opened them, and she could see how enthralled he was with her body. He stroked her shoulder, and Simon squeezed against her. She glanced down and saw Caden sitting in the chair. He was naked and watching them, like he was watching over them.

She felt guilty. She couldn't let this go too far. Not right now anyway. They would be in danger. If her secret was revealed, they would be more protective of her, and it would cause conflict. Plus if she had to leave, if she had to do a mission or overseas trip for months, she would have to continue to lie. Her heart was heavy. She lifted up.

Simon gripped her hip.

"Where are you going?" he asked. Caden sat forward. Aqua lifted up to lean on his elbow.

"I should go freshen up, and maybe you could grab my dress," she suggested, but then Caden eased out of the chair and knelt onto the bed.

He slid his palm over her ankle and shook his head. "You don't need to leave, to run from what we're all feeling. Don't think about tomorrow or next week. Just enjoy tonight. It's been perfect," he said and pulled her lower until her ass was at the edge of the bed, and he eased over her. He looked so intense. Her lips parted, her pussy clenched with need, and she thought about how it felt having three men inside of her at once. She wanted it again and again.

His hand slid up her ankle and calf, then to her thigh and her breast. "Arms up," he said to her, surprising her. When she didn't immediately do it, he raised one eyebrow up at her. She slowly complied, then watched him, didn't take her eyes off of him even his palm slid over her breast and he used the pad of his thumb to tease her nipple. She lifted her pelvis.

"You're not going anywhere, woman. You've gotten under our skin, have given us a little taste of you, and we want more." He slid one thigh between her legs. His knee was against her pussy as he lowered down, cupped her cheeks, and began to kiss her. His kisses were tender, sweet, and then demanding. His body was thick, filled with muscles, and she knew he was capable and strong.

She slid her hands to his shoulders, and then through his hair when he lifted up, grabbed them, and pressed them down against the comforter.

Her legs were wide against his thick hips. His cock was now at her pussy, but instead of thrusting into her, he explored her body with his mouth. He tapped her hands and gave her a stern look, indicating to stay put. She did. She was turned on by him, by his command. He lowered down her body, licked her breast, tugged on her nipple, and her pussy clenched. He swirled his tongue around the areola as his brothers watched, and then their hands pressed over hers, palms to palms. She lifted her torso against Caden's belly, and he went lower and lower, slid his tongue into her cunt, and then lifted her thighs. He pulled her a little further down as he stood now, her ass and cunt off the bed. "Look at our woman, brothers. She's ours, and she's so very special. Let's show her who's in charge," he said, and that was it. It was sensation overload as he thrust his cock right into her cunt while Simon and Aqua held her hands above her head and began to feast on her breasts. They tugged and pulled, swirled their tongues over each nipple, and she was powerless, under their control, their restraints.

"Oh God, please. Please, Caden, Simon, Aqua, oh!" She cried out and came.

"Together," Caden commanded.

"Ours," Aqua said, and then Caden pulled out of her. Simon and Aqua released their holds, and Caden lifted her up and against him. He kissed her, and she kissed him back, feeling wild and needy for more. Then he set her feet down, turned her around, and pressed her over the edge of the bed. He slid his cock into her cunt from behind and pressed into her.

She moaned. "Yes."

He thrust faster, deeper, and held his palm under her hair to her neck, restraining her, and she came hard and fast.

"Ready," Simon said, and then Caden pulled out of her and lifted her up, pulled her into his arms, and kissed her again. Then he fell to the bed on his back, and she straddled him. Their lips parted, and she immediately took his cock into her cunt. She sank down, and they both moaned. He reached up and tugged her hair and then cupped her cheek. "Never like this. Never. This is special," he said, and she lowered down to kiss him, not wanting to think about how serious his words were or his tone.

Smack.

She gasped, but Caden kept kissing her.

"This is the sexiest ass I've ever seen. I can't wait to fuck it and smack it," Aqua said, and April was shocked. Not only by Aqua's words but his actions he—

Smack.

Smack.

She moaned and then felt the cool liquid hit her asshole. Fingers slid in and out, and she felt her pussy come. She wanted it. Needed it. Craved to be taken by them, possessed like this by them. She pulled her mouth from Caden's as Aqua replaced fingers with his cock.

"Mine," he said so powerfully and then slid into her ass.

"Aqua," she cried out.

"Your mouth now," Simon demanded.

She looked at him through hooded eyes, lifted up as Aqua and Caden stroked into her cunt and her ass. She was overwhelmed with emotion and with her body's reaction to being possessed like this. She opened to Simon. His cock was long, hard, and pre-cum dripped from the tip. She licked it, and he hissed.

He gripped her hair. "Not letting you go. You're staying the night, hell, the fucking weekend. This mouth is incredible. You're incredible."

"She sure is. I'm there, baby. Fuck, I'm there," Aqua said, and then he thrust into her ass and came. She moaned against Simon's cock and bobbed her head up and down. She was overwhelmed with emotions. Shocked to feel so much. She never felt this much about anyone.

"There. Coming. Fuck," Simon said and rocked his hips and came. She swallowed his cum, licked him clean, and didn't want to release him when he moaned and pulled away. "Jesus, woman," he exclaimed and fell back. Simon chuckled, but Caden was still feeling a bit possessive or maybe afraid that she might leave them. He rolled her to her back and thrust into her hard and fast. He held her head under his forearm and rocked his hips. Their gazes locked, and she came again.

"Oh...oh!" she cried out.

"April." He clenched his teeth and then roared as he came inside of her. He fell against her, nearly crushing her, but she wrapped her legs around his waist and held on to him. He kissed her neck and suckled on a sensitive spot. She gasped and giggled, and he kept it up as he lifted and she swatted at his arm. Her breasts pressed against his pectoral muscles, and he stroked her hair from her face. "Stay the night. Don't go home," he said to her so softly, yet with a look of determination and as if it were an order and she would be crazy to deny it.

"You want me to? You're sure?"

"Fuck yeah," Aqua said. She glanced at him, and he winked at her. Then she felt Caden's fingertip under her chin, making her look at him again.

"Say yes," he said.

She hesitated only a moment.

"Yes," she replied, and he pressed his mouth to hers and then eased from her cunt, slid to the side, and took her with him.

"Nice," Simon said as Caden took the spot Simon had before.

"Learn to share, bro," Aqua said.

"Easy for you to say. You didn't lose your spot," he said, and Caden cleared his throat.

"Round three, you get top," he said. Her cheeks felt warm, and she kissed Caden's chest, thinking about what he said and how they would make love again tonight. Well, at this rate, she might be staying the weekend. She might not be able to walk.

Chapter Five

Mike was feeling a little bit buzzed, but Katie, the redhead he picked up in the bar, was all over him. She was definitely a little drunk, but they hit it off well and spent the evening alone at the bar, bullshitting and making out like they knew one another for a while. It was time to take her home and whatever happened. This night turned out a hell of a lot better than he thought. He really wasn't sure if Cynthia would buy the routine that April was his date and his lover he replaced Cynthia with, but she did. He owed April big time for going along with it. Especially since she liked Caden, Simon, and Aqua, and they were ready to kill him over her. He chuckled. April wouldn't know what hit her with those three badass Seals staking a claim. He could feel the attraction between them and April. It was magical, and he couldn't help but to be envious.

He pulled Katie into his arms and pressed her against the car door as he kissed her. He knew this wasn't going to turn into anything, or maybe it might. He had no expectations and was just going to go with the flow. She moaned into his mouth, and he felt her up, cupped her decent-size breasts, and then stroked the nipples. He moved his mouth over her neck, and she gripped him tight.

"Holy crap, Mike. I can't believe how you make me feel," she said, and her words made him wince a little. Would it be a dick move to fuck her and leave her? Was he just trying to protect his heart after what Cynthia did to him?

"We got tonight, baby. I feel it, too," he admitted and cupped her cheeks, looked into her light green eyes, and he felt something. A twinge of something he didn't want to face. He pulled back and winked, covering up the connection.

"Let's go. Where do you live?"

Not far from here," she said.

"Hey, Mike, have a good night, buddy!" Vince yelled to him, walking away with a blonde on his arm. She was kissing Vince's neck, and Vince had his hand on her ass as they headed to his car.

"Good night," Mike said and then got Katie into the car. He drove down the road and headed to her place with her sliding her palm up and down his inner thigh then over his cock.

"Oh, Mike," she whispered then leaned closer to kiss his neck. He knew he was hung big, and Cynthia loved that about him, or so he thought. He blinked his eyes, focused on driving when he probably shouldn't be driving. He was pretty buzzed. He got to her place, and they giggled and tripped a little. Now that the alcohol was absorbing into his system, he felt a little more buzzed, but they got into her place, a townhouse that was pretty nice. She walked over to the bar and poured them some shots. She clicked on some music, and he smiled, pulled her next to him, and then they clicked glasses and drank. They drank some more, and she swayed her hips to the music as he began to kiss her and undress her right there. She reached for the bottle and then led him to her bedroom. He stumbled for a second, and they laughed. Then she put the bottle on the dresser by the bed, and he lifted her up and dropped her onto the bed, his knee between her legs, her dress to her waist, and her full breasts exposed.

"You're fucking hot, baby. You've made my night."

"Make mine, Mike, and fuck me." His dick hardened, and he kissed her hard on the mouth while cupping her breast and then slid the dress the rest of the way off of her. She lay there before him like a feast. Her long red hair cascaded over the comforter, her light green eyes sparkled, and she widened her thighs and lifted her pussy toward him.

"Please, Mike," she said, and he gave her a wink, quickly undressed despite the dizziness in his head, and made certain she would never forget him or tonight ever.

* * * *

April was in the shower finishing up. She couldn't believe the depth of the emotions she was feeling. It was crazy, but it seemed that Caden, Aqua, and Simon were penetrating that wall she built up over her heart. She fought for years to build it up. To protect her from the pain of loss, of losing those she cared about, and being human. How could one night, several times making love, do this to her?

She finished up, turned off the water, then grabbed the towel to dry off. Her head was spinning. What should she do? How should she handle this?

She realized she had nothing to wear. She didn't know where her dress was, so she kept the towel wrapped around her body, dried her hair, and then walked out of the bathroom. The room was empty, the sheets and comforter fixed. Maybe they were ready for her to leave, too. She couldn't believe the disappointed, sad, and angry feelings she had. Then Caden walked into the bedroom, buttoning up his uniform shirt.

"Morning," he said to her, gazing over her standing there in the towel.

"Morning. Do you have my dress so I can get out of your hair?" she asked with an attitude even she heard in her tone.

He squinted and then stopped buttoning his shirt, closed the space between them, making her take a retreating step back, but he grabbed the towel and her and pulled her against him. "We aren't kicking you out. I have to go to work. The fair is today on the boardwalk and pier. Simon and Aqua will take you home to change, and then you guys will meet me there." He stared into her eyes and then reached up and stroked her jaw and chin, tilting it up toward him.

She was shocked by his order, like she was supposed to just go to this fair with them because they said so. It would mean her friends knowing that she slept with them, and that would mean more people involved, more emotions and a connection. Her heart began to pound in her chest. She pulled away and wouldn't look at him.

"I'm not sure I can make it. I have some things to do for work and calls to make." She was putting up the walls. Even she knew it was obvious.

"Don't do that. Don't minimize last night and this morning."

"What's going on?" Aqua asked, coming into the room with her dress. She walked toward him.

"Nothing. Thanks, I'll be a minute, and then we can go. You can drop me off at home." She took the dress from him. She walked over toward the other side of the bed, her back toward them as she dropped the towel and reached for the dress. She got it up over her hips and then started to reach back for the one string to clip behind her neck when Caden's hands covered hers.

"Let me," he said, and then she felt his body against hers. The material of his uniform shirt and pants aroused her skin on her back. She felt his lips against her neck and shoulder.

"Don't push us away. We'll go slow if that's what you need. We want you with us today. I need to see you with my brothers and know that last night meant something to you."

"Meant something to all of us," Aqua said, stepping in front of her, placing his hand on her hips, then sliding them up to cup her breasts.

"Aqua, please."

Caden gripped her hair under her neck and pressed against her back. She felt his hard cock hit her spine.

"This wasn't just sex, and we all know it. You're panicked over it, and I don't know why, but I'll find out why when you share it with us. Tonight, after this fair, we'll come over and spend some more time together." Aqua released her to Caden, and she turned sideways.

"I told you that my life is crazy right now. The timing was bad."

He shook his head.

"We'll work it out. We aren't letting you go, April. This is too fucking perfect." He pressed his lips to hers, and she was overwhelmed with emotions she didn't want to give in to. But it seemed like they were going to be as stubborn as she was being. When he released her lips, Aqua pulled her into his arms and kissed her next. She held on to his shoulders as he dipped her and slid his hand under her dress right to her ass. He stroked the crack with his finger, and she moaned into his mouth. They had each taken her there several times last night. They made love to her together, infused their mark on her together, and the depth of their connection was like nothing she ever felt before. When Aqua released her lips and removed his hand, Simon was there. His hands were on his hips, his eyebrows crinkled, his muscles bulging from the tight T-shirt in navy blue he wore with a pair of jeans.

"Come to me, April," he commanded. She swallowed hard, glanced at Caden and Aqua, who were looking at her with firm expressions, and for some reason she was aroused, wet all over again.

"Someone needs more convincing to know we mean business," Caden said.

Smack. She gasped and reached back as Caden smacked her ass, locked gazes with her, and winked. "I'll see the three of you later," he said and walked from the bedroom.

"The convincing starts now," Aqua said and reached for her dress, lifted it from her body, and then pulled her into his arms and began to kiss her. He fell to the bed, and she kissed him back, turned on once again by their dominance and control.

Then she felt Simon behind her. He massaged her ass. "When I give you an order, you best do it without hesitation." Smack.

Smack.

Smack.

He spanked her ass and then slid a finger into her cunt. She moaned into Aqua's mouth.

"Someone needs step-by-step instructions," he said.

She heard his zipper go down, and then Aqua released her lips. "We want you. Every fucking second, every minute, all the fucking time," he told her, and she stared at him and felt herself get emotional. He squinted.

"This is new to me, Aqua. I don't get involved with men," she said.

"Well, you're involved now, and things are changing, so accept it, and accept us. We won't hurt you, baby. We promise," Aqua said as he held her cheeks between his hands. She stared at him and then she felt the cool liquid press into her asshole.

"Simon." She hissed.

"Convincing starts now."

He pulled his fingers from her ass and replaced them with his cock. She moaned and lowered her head to Aqua's chest as he caressed her hair and thrust his hips upward. They were at it again. Making love to her again. Possessing her body where no man had ever possessed before. With every stroke into her ass, and every grunt and moan from Simon, she felt her heart grow fonder for them, for this relationship and what it could turn into. Could she let go and entertain such a relationship and connection? Was her heart, her soul capable of it? She didn't know and could no longer analyze her emotions. She wanted them inside of her together. The only thing that would make it perfect would be Caden inside her, too.

She lifted up as Aqua undid his pants and helped him push them down. Simon assisted, holding his cock in her ass, and his thick, muscular arm around her waist lifted her a moment as Aqua shoved them down. Then he was lying there naked, fisting his cock and licking his lips.

"Ride him, sweetheart. You're ours, and we aren't letting you go," Simon said. She sunk down over Aqua's cock, wanting him, needing to feel more of that sensation of being possessed, marked, and owned by them. They began to thrust in sync, destroying her resistance and once again making her feel things so deeply she felt tears in her eyes and nearly cried. She pulled it together, knowing she couldn't make them ask more questions, but perhaps she could let them in a little more than she thought. With every stroke and every thrust, she fell deeper, and her aching heart opened up a little bit more.

* * * *

"This is one hell of a house, April. My God, it's stunning, and this view, wow," Simon said as he and Aqua walked outside and looked toward the ocean. He was so impressed with her place, and it seemed she was well off. He felt a bit below her despite the fact that he and his brothers were well off, too. They lived in a house they had shared throughout their military careers. It had originally been an investment property their parents owned, and they bought from them. They owned other rentals in the area, as well, so they were doing pretty good financially, but it seemed their woman was wealthy. It surprised him. She was so down to earth, sweet, and quiet.

"Thank you. I have drinks and things in the refrigerator. Help yourselves while I freshen up and change."

"We have time," Aqua said to her, and she gave a soft smile before walking back into the house and toward her bedroom. Simon watched her. Her body was exceptional.

"Holy shit, bro, this place is exquisite. I think she's really well off," Aqua said and swallowed hard. His brother was obviously feeling just like Simon was.

"She's so down to earth, though, and sweet. Maybe modest about her successes, and that's why she's so secretive," Simon replied and began to look around the patio and the walkway that led down to the beach.

"I don't know. You heard what Watson and the guys said about April helping Amelia with self-defense training and relaxation techniques," Aqua added.

"So she knows self-defense. You heard her last night with Ice. Her dad was a cop and a Marine. She's prepared, and she's a single woman living alone and travels a lot. She probably wants to be prepared just in case," Simon added.

"You see this?" Aqua asked, moving the branches back from the stone walls that overlooked the beach below. Simon squinted and saw the camera.

"Damn, Fogerty was right. He said she had high-tech surveillance cameras installed by some friends."

"Yeah, guy friends, and not sure if you noticed, but she has no tan lines," Aqua pointed out. Simon felt jealous.

"We can't ponder over anything she did with anyone before us," Simon told him.

"We can tell her no more sunbathing in the nude unless one of us are with her," Aqua said firmly.

His brother was definitely feeling possessive, and Simon couldn't blame him. The woman rocked their world in one fucking night.

When April emerged, Simon's heart pounded inside of his chest. She looked beautiful, dressed in a one-piece, slim-fitting tank dress in black, with heeled sandals and her hair pulled up in some fancy style with wisps of pieces falling here and there. She wore a heart pendant necklace, and the heart fell right at the dip of deep cleavage of her breasts. More was exposed as she bent down to fix the strap on her sandals.

"Damn, woman, maybe we should stay here and forget about the fair," Aqua told her, closing the space between them and pulling her into his arms. The sight aroused Simon, of course, as well as how his brother's palm slid over her ass and squeezed.

"Caden will be angry," she said, and Aqua squeezed her ass and then nuzzled next to her neck.

"But you love his ass spankings. Bet he would give you one for not showing up,"

She closed her eyes, and Simon licked his lip and joined them. "She'll get one anyway, and Caden will come up with a reason why," he said, and Aqua chuckled as he stepped back, releasing her to Simon.

"Nice," she replied and went to turn. Simon snagged her wrist, and she stopped to look at him.

"You're stunning in everything you wear, but all I want to do is unwrap you." He reached up, cupped her cheek, and then drew her closer so he could kiss her. He hugged her to him, and she hugged him back.

"We should go," she said, and he exhaled.

"Fine," he replied, and she pulled back and smiled.

"Let me just lock up," she said and pulled out her cell phone, and they watched the sliders close up and then the shades pull halfway.

"Impressive. You have the security done professionally?" Aqua asked as they headed out of her home. When the door closed, she hit another button on her phone, and they heard the locks engage.

"Yes. I have many wealthy clients in various businesses. We worked out a deal," she said, and Simon felt a bit jealous again. His thoughts were going in crazy directions. Was she part of the deal? Did she sleep with these clients? Fuck, he was losing his cool. He wasn't used to this line of thinking at all.

Aqua opened the door, and Simon lifted her up into his arms to help her into the truck.

"I can get up into the truck alone, you know. My heels aren't too high," she said.

"Maybe I like picking you up and holding you close," he said to her, and she exhaled.

"What? You don't like it?" he asked, climbing in next to her. He closed the door, and Aqua began to drive.

"I'm just not used to it, that's all. I take care of myself." She crossed her legs.

Aqua placed his hand on her knee and squeezed it. "Times are changing, baby. No more fending for yourself. Oh, and no more laying out naked to sunbathe either," he added, and Simon snickered.

"What?" she asked him as he drove down her driveway and then down the sandy road.

"You didn't think we would notice you don't have any tan lines?" Simon asked her.

She shrugged her shoulders. "No one can see me. I own six acres of property, and I face the ocean."

Simon placed his hand on her thigh and eased up under her skirt. "Not anymore. With one of us nearby watching over you, never alone."

"That's rather presumptuous of you, Mr. Farmer," she said to him.

"Not at all."

"Well, I don't know what types of women you're used to, but I'm pretty independent, and I don't take orders well."

"Nothing a firm hand won't resolve," Aqua said, and she gasped.

"Or three Seals," Simon added, and she shook her head and exhaled in frustration. He couldn't help but to smile. Never in his life would he think he would meet a woman his brothers and he could share and feel so perfect. With April he wanted everything, and he wanted it instantly. April, on the other hand, was going to fight it tooth and nail, and as much as he wondered why and got a funny feeling of concern, he also felt aroused and ready to break down her resistance and claim her their woman. She was perfect.

* * * *

"What do you have for me, Kulta?" Victoria asked over the phone.

"There was a little confusion in our first observations last night."

"What do you mean?"

"The blonde isn't with the agent. She left with the chief of police."

"What?"

"Yeah, Waters left with a redhead later in the evening and was with her all night at her place. Those pictures I sent are of the redhead at the bar and then up against the car."

"Shit."

"Where is Waters now?"

"Still with the redhead."

"What is his relationship with the blonde then?"

"Seems to be just friends. I had some men check out her place. It's got some nice security. Pretty high-tech."

"Well, from what our people found out initially, she works for a finance and banking agency in New York, travels often. I'm going to dig deeper. Make sure those men don't get caught."

"I pulled the team already. The place is accessible if and when the time comes."

"Good. Now about the redhead, if he's still with her into the afternoon, get me what you can on her, too. She may come in handy, as well."

"You got it."

She ended the call and then looked at Gorbin and Fulta.

"I want everything we can get on this blonde. The more I'm finding out, the more interesting she becomes. I have a feeling that Rosen may find her to be pretty appealing, as well. In fact, I may need to call him sooner than later and explain."

"I thought you wanted to surprise him?" Gorbin asked.

"I did, and I'm still not sure. Wondering how she knows Mike so well."

"Maybe from that bar everyone hangs out at, and the friends they keep."

"Maybe. Dig deeper. I want anything you can get."

"Got it."

* * * *

Caden kept looking at his watch. Where the hell were Simon, Aqua, and April? He couldn't wait to see her. It was unnerving how much he liked her. He was talking to different people, pretending to be focused, when she came into sight. He literally stopped talking to Zayn Stelling.

"Ahhh, so that's what your bad mood is about. You missed your woman," Zayn said, and the fact that he picked up on his attitude as well as the way he said "your woman" got under Caden's skin quickly. But then April locked gazes with him and headed over with Aqua and Simon.

"Hi," she said to Zayn and kissed his cheek hello first, and it kind of angered Caden. He wanted her, waited for her to get here, but she was obviously trying to act like they hadn't slept with her last night. He wanted everyone to know she was his and his brothers', despite promising her to go slow.

"Good to see you. Have you been here long?" Zayn asked.

"A little while," Simon said and shook Zayn's hand.

"April," Caden said. She stepped toward him, and he caressed along her hip to her ass and pulled her into his arms. He kissed her softly on the lips then released them. "Thought you might not show," he whispered.

Her feminine hands were against his chest, and she licked her lips.

"Not a chance with these two," she replied and glanced at Simon.

He placed his hand on her shoulder and squeezed. "She's a bit recalcitrant, Chief. Doesn't take orders well at all," he said. Her face went flushed, and Zayn chuckled.

"Congratulations, guys," Zayn said, smiling, and then he walked away, leaving them alone.

"Caden, we talked about this."

"Yeah, well, I missed you, and you look hot, and I want everyone to know you're taken." He pulled her close again and kissed her tenderly. She heard some whistles, and then he slowly released her and winked.

"Nice," she said through clenched teeth.

"Just wait." He winked, and she shook her head and exhaled.

* * * *

April found it difficult to ignore the pull to touch them or be close to them. She held on to Simon's hand right now as they walked around and talked to people. They joined Kai and her men for lunch and then were talking about where to go next when her cell phone rang. She opened her purse and looked down, seeing the number and knowing it was Pierre.

"Can you please excuse me a minute? It's work related, and I need to take the call. It's overseas," she said to Simon, and he nodded. She smiled at him and then the others and answered the call, walking away. A quick glance over her shoulder and Simon, Caden, and Aqua watched her, but then Kai and the men asked them something and they smiled and started talking.

"Hi."

"Bad timing?" Pierre asked.

"I'm at the fair."

"With the Seals?"

"And others."

He chuckled.

"Well, something is going on. Not sure what yet."

Her heart began to race. She glanced again at the men, but their backs were toward her. She remained close to the railing overlooking the beach, and no one was near her.

"Okay, I'm alone. Talk to me," she said to him.

"Someone is snooping around, looking for info on you. Don't know if it's those Seals or someone else."

She felt the ache in her chest and then anger.

"Are you serious?"

"Listen, I don't think it's the Seals. Things aren't coming from any direction that would indicate that, but we're trying to pinpoint from where. You know these things take some serious digging."

"Jesus, Pierre, what do I do? No one has even tried to look me up or investigate me."

"We have your cover in place. You know your shit, so stick with it."

"Keep lying to these men? I can't do this."

"You care about them?"

"Shit." She exhaled, and when she looked back toward the men, they looked concerned. She forced a smile and then held her finger up indicating she needed more time. "Don't panic."

"I am panicking because if it isn't them and someone else, someone involved with the case, then I could put them and anyone else in danger."

"I don't think there's a need to panic."

"This is what I was afraid of. Listen, get things set for me to leave for New York tonight."

"Are you sure?"

"Yes, I'm sure and make it look good. Set me up at the Ritz Carlton. The best of everything and bring in some posers. Someone wants to look into my business dealings and who I am, then we can give them a show. Make sure those posers are legitimate. Send me their files. I'll look them over and approve them."

"I know your requirements. I'll make it happen and send your arrangements through the business link, so if anyone is really digging, they'll get that through the email we have set up."

"Excellent. I need to go."

"Don't worry. Enjoy the rest of the day with them."

"I'll try."

She ended the call as the three men watched her and looked like they were coming over. She pretended to look at her email off the phone as she made the fake call. Simon, Aqua, and Caden walked over. She covered the mouthpiece.

"Give me a minute. I got a call, and I need to leave for business tonight," she said and saw their surprised expressions. The person on the other end answered.

"Hi, Dave, it's April. Yeah, I just heard from Nate, and he's ready to negotiate the terms of the contract. I know it's making everyone upset and antsy to close this thing, but we're talking ten million. He wants to meet us and go over this deal to ensure it's in his best interest to invest. I think now is the time to talk to Kevin and get him to give a little more. He wants this to happen. It's good all around, and we each make out well." She glanced at her watch. "I know Nate trusts my judgment, so I'm willing to jump on a plane and get there to help seal the deal. Can you get in in touch with the pilot? I'm hoping to leave around seven this evening. I have plans with friends I'm not willing to break right now, and I don't want this guy thinking he has that control that I'll jump when he snaps his fingers," she said, knowing the men were listening and hoping they were buying her act. She wanted them to accept her taking off like this because of work. Her mind was already jumping to finding out who the hell was trying to find out information on her and why.

The man on the other end, an agent, replied to her, and she lipped "I'm sorry" to the guys.

"Okay, so the car will pick me up at six tonight? Great. Yes, I hope so, too. Keep me posted on the arrangements and things. I'll touch base a little later to make sure things are set and then again tonight on the plane. Okay."

She ended the call and then exhaled. "I'm so sorry."

"We heard. Where do you have to fly out to?" Caden asked.

"New York," she replied.

"How long will you be gone?" Simon asked.

"Not sure. Depends on this client and how negotiations go. It's been one hell of a process. Over six months and every time we get close to completing this deal, something comes up. Forget it, I'm ranting. I just want this project closed so I can focus on other things, and other negotiations. I also have a few other business trips coming up overseas, and I want to handle them with a clear mind." She closed her eyes and exhaled then felt Simon wrap his arm around her waist and hug her from behind. She exhaled and leaned back.

"Relax and it will work out fine. You seem very focused and successful," he said and kissed her neck.

She was once again confused. Could they be the ones looking into her background? God, why did that bother her so much when she did the same on them? She knew a lot about them as far as their military experiences. She could have dug deeper. Maybe she should. Maybe she should ask Pierre about what else he found out about them that she told him not to share.

Aqua took her hand and brought it to his lips. He kissed her knuckles. "So a car service is picking you up at six?" he asked.

"Yes. I have some things to do before that though. I think you guys should drop me off at home. I need to pack and then gather some files and things on the computer and talk to my team about meeting tonight when I get to New York. It's going to be a long night for me." She felt Simon squeeze her a little tighter.

"What time can you get out of here, Chief?" Simon asked and continued to kiss her neck.

"Another hour tops. I'll work it out so we can spend a couple of more hours with April before she needs to get ready," he said then stepped closer, gripped her chin, tilted it up toward him, then kissed her.

When he released her lips, Aqua pulled her into his arms and hugged her. She hugged him back and held Caden's gaze. "I have a lot to do."

"We're going to need a few things to hold us over until you return to us, baby," he said, and his eyes roamed over her body before he winked.

"Let me go wrap things up. I'll meet you at your house in an hour," Caden said then put his sunglasses on and walked away. Aqua ran his palm along her ass, and Simon pressed up against her back. She was sandwiched between them.

He rubbed up her arm to her shoulder then neck. "We'll hang out with Kai and them a little longer and then head out. We're going to miss you, baby," he told her. She stepped back, and they partially released her. Aqua kept a hand at her hip, and Simon rubbed her back.

"I'll miss you guys, too, but remember what I said. I have a busy life and career. This won't be the last time I have to leave for business."

"We'll work it out," Aqua said.

"Yes, we'll work it out," Simon added.

* * * *

"What's wrong? You seem preoccupied," Zayn asked Caden right before he was getting ready to leave for the day and go to April's. His mind was heavy on some things she said and her need to not share so much.

"Just things on my mind."

"Anything I can help with?" Zayn asked.

Caden looked around them. "I don't think so. Just trying to work things through in my head.'

"Ahh, April."

Caden looked at him and squinted.

"It hits you out of nowhere. The possessiveness, the jealousy and protectiveness, then the questions and worry. I know what you're going through. It will get better as you all build that trust," Zayn told him.

"Kind of hard when she's holding back."

"Like you aren't, too?" he asked.

"No, we really aren't. Under normal circumstances, we'd hold our guard up, but with her it's different. This whole thing is."

Zany nodded. "Totally get it. We're all military, all been through heavy shit and have trained our minds, our hearts to be so strong and under guard. Then we meet someone, and suddenly we're ready to express feelings and a vulnerability that is unheard of. Rocks the mind, man, and even makes you feel on edge, snappy even."

"Definitely snappy. I feel like when I talk to her, I'm giving orders." He laughed.

"Been there and I still do it, but Kai seems to get it."

"Yeah, well, for some reason I feel like April does, too, but she's also defiant. I think it's her independence. She lives alone, seems to have a guard over her heart."

"Well, it's all new man. It just started. You can't get her life story in twenty- four hours."

"You're right. Now she has to leave for business."

"Ahhh, so you're going to miss her and you're in a pissed-off mood."

"Pretty much. She doesn't share much about her work either."

"She makes good money. Must with the place she has. Heard it's sweet."

"I haven't seen it, but my brothers were impressed."

"Maybe that's what's bothering you. She's all business professional and well off, and seems like she doesn't need a man or men to take care of her."

"I was thinking that, too, but my gut is telling me there's more."

"Well, I'm sure you checked her out."

"Not yet."

"Well, maybe you should, and that might help."

"I don't want to do that. It's like asking her to trust us and then not trusting her. Maybe I can get more out of her tonight."

"If not, then when she returns. Maybe take advantage of the time before she leaves to enforce the power of the connection the four of you have. That could help a lot."

"Look at you, our guru on romance," Caden teased.

"Fuck you, you know I'm right."

"Yeah, you are. Thanks, buddy."

"Hey, we men have to stick together."

"Ain't that the truth."

Chapter Six

"Caden!" April screamed his name as he thrust into her ass from behind. She was holding on to Simon, trying to ride him at the same time. Aqua had just come in her mouth and now lay on her king-size bedspread out and gasping for breath.

Caden gripped her hair and rocked into her deeper, faster. "Fuck, I'm going to miss you, baby and this perfect ass." He stroked faster, and then Simon cursed.

"Fuck, I can't take it. I'm there, baby. There." He grunted as he came. Caden wrapped his arm around her waist and lifted her off of Simon. Simon moaned, and then Caden set her feet down on the floor by the edge of the bed, pressed her down so her chest hit the comforter.

"Arms out above you," he ordered, and she came from his orders and his control.

Her breasts were pressed to the comforter, her thighs spread as he thrust into her asshole. She felt his palms slide over her ass and then up her back. When he gripped the back of her neck and hair and leaned over her, she couldn't take it. "Caden, oh God, Caden, you're wild."

"And you're so fucking giving. I love restraining you, having you under my control and command. Do you like that, April?" he asked and rocked his cock in and out of her ass.

"Yes, oh yes, I do."

"Good girl."

"Holy shit," Aqua said and covered her one hand she had laying above her. Her face was pressed to the comforter, and she was completely at Caden's mercy.

Smack.

Smack. Smack.

"Oh God." She moaned and came some more as he spanked her ass then thrust into her again and again.

"Think about this when you're away from us. Think about us being your men and the fact that you're our woman, and when you get back, I want you naked, pressed over the bed, offering us this pussy, this ass, and this sexy mouth."

Smack, smack, smack.

She cried out and came.

"Fuck," he said and thrust three more times, then growled as he came in her ass. He waited to catch his breath, and she couldn't even move. She felt his cock slide from her ass, and he shivered, then leaned down and began to kiss her shoulders, her spine, and each ass cheek.

"Take care of her and I'll be right back," he said. She felt Simon and Aqua's hands on her skin, massaging her.

"You don't know how long you'll be away for?" Simon asked her.

She looked at him and lifted up. "A few days maybe."

He looked angry, but then he gave a soft smile and caressed her cheek. Caden returned with a washcloth and rolled her to her back, pressed his thigh between her legs, and she watched him. She didn't dare reach for the towel, or he would give her that stern expression and tell her it was their responsibility to take care of her and to protect her. She swallowed hard. This was going to be so hard. She really hoped they hadn't investigated her, and then she hoped they did because that meant no one from her past had and perhaps they weren't in danger.

He tossed the towel onto the floor and then slid over her once again. She straddled his waist, ran her palms up and down his chest.

"I have to start getting ready."

He nodded then pressed his lips to hers. When he got up, Aqua took his place. He pulled her toward him, and she straddled his waist then hugged him. He ran his palm along her ass and back, caressing her, and she absorbed his cologne, the trim muscles he had all over his chest, and she kissed his neck and then his lips. Then she went to Simon. He immediately pulled her into his arms and kissed her breathless. She raised her thigh up against his hip, and he stroked a finger up into her cunt. She grabbed onto his shoulders. "Simon.'

"Shhh, just another feel. I love watching you come. Watching those sexy green eyes sparkle then flutter." He thrust faster, and she gripped his shoulders and let go. She held his gaze as he ordered her to, and then he changed his mind. He pulled out his finger and replaced it with his cock. He rolled her fully to her back and slid right in, held her one leg up against his side, and rocked down into her. Her breasts were against his mouth, her head tilted back, and he rocked so hard, so deeply she cried out her release. "So fucking gorgeous. I'll never get enough, baby. Never," he said and then came. He hugged her to him, and she held his head against her chest as he suckled her nipple and tugged. She closed her eyes and absorbed being here with them, making love to them several times in just a couple of hours. Had she made the right decision to leave for a few days, or would she regret it completely?

* * * *

"April is in New York. Someone has been trying to find out information on her, and I just confirmed that it wasn't those Navy Seals," Pierre told Mike over the phone.

"Shit, this isn't good. She was looking into those businessmen. She got shit on that guy, Ferrin."

"I know, and I'm in touch with our people and making plans. I'm debating about pulling April, but I think she'll fight me on it. Where are you now?"

"Meeting a friend for lunch."

"Oh, you, too, huh. Must be that town. Can you send over what you got from the team there investigating those imports coming from Saudi Arabia? I got a guy who caught wind of a phone call between someone in Syria and a person running a business in Germany."

"Shit, I got several leads going on two men from both those places. They may be involved with something together."

"That's what we're thinking. I'm calling the colonel next. His teams are ready to go and moving into positions so they can jump in and assist."

"How is April holding up?"

"Her focus is protecting those Seals, and she felt that doing this last-minute business trip would serve several purposes, including throwing them off to give a little breathing room. She really likes them."

"Well, they really like her. I thought they were going to kill me for pretending she was my date."

Pierre chuckled. "This is going to be rough for her. If she does care about them, then she'll want to protect them any way she can. I'd say going in the field ever again isn't going to happen."

"I get that feeling, too. I'll get on this, and make a call now before I meet my lunch date."

"Enjoy and I'll touch base later."

Mike ended the call and glanced around the parking lot. Katie was meeting him there before she had to go to work. He wasn't going to ask her to lunch. Not so soon, but he stayed with her for the weekend and figured he would take things slow. He made the call, keeping eyes out for her and wondering if anything could come of this. Thinking about the position he did for the government under the state police, he wondered if he could pull back, as well. This town was getting to him, and also helping him to feel like he could have the things other men had. Was he rushing this? Looking at this too deeply? Katie was sweet, and she was younger than him. She was pretty, had a good job at the hospital as a nurse, and she did it for him in bed. He smiled, made the calls, and even looked at emails and then at his watch. Where was Katie? She was twenty minutes late.

* * * *

Caden was working and driving along the side streets heading back to the department when the call came over the radio. There had been a break-in at the condos not far from where he was. He called into the department as he headed to the scene and got the low down.

"What's the deal?" he asked.

"Well, Chief, we have two officers who arrived on the scene initially at the request of a break-in at one of the condos. Water was running from the condo above and leaking through the ceiling below. Officers on scene say there looks to have been a struggle, and no sign of the tenant, a female by the name of Katie Roark."

"Katie Roark?" He knew that Katie had been with Mike Waters Friday night. They seemed to have hit it off well, and April mentioned him liking her.

"Anything else?" he asked.

"Blood on the rug leading to the door. Just a few spots."

"I'm on my way."

Caden pulled into the parking lot, and the police were on scene. Behind him came an unmarked police car, and he knew that the state police were called in. He followed them up, the area taped off so no one could contaminate any evidence. He saw what they did, a definite struggle. There was a shoe in the bathroom on the floor. The tub was turned off as water was overflowing and going down to the condo below. That was what initiated the call. Through further investigation, it was obvious that Katie was taken. Her purse and phone were on the table, and it was going off. Several texts could be seen, including two from Mike. He assumed it was Mike Waters. He pulled out his cell phone. "Mike, it's Caden. Is Katie with you?"

"No, I was supposed to meet her at the diner. I've been sitting here for thirty minutes, and she isn't answering her phone."

"Mike, I'm at her condo. Get over here. The detectives are going to have questions. It looks like someone took her."

* * * *

Mike was beside himself. What in the world was going on? How did this happen? Who took her? Where the hell was she, and what was going on? He answered the detectives' questions. They knew him, and he worked inside the state police barracks. He told them to be thorough to ensure they knew he was telling the truth. He gave them any info he had and realized it was very little. "This would have been a first date today. We were together over the weekend. All small talk but made plans for after her shift at the hospital. She called this morning and said she would go to sleep after lunch because she worked all night."

"We'll get to the bottom of this. We're contacting her friends and seeing if there were any ex-boyfriends, or any threats toward her, anything we can get."

"She's so sweet and very soft-spoken. I couldn't imagine her having any enemies," Mike said as they stood outside of the condo in the parking lot. Mike's cell phone rang. He looked down. "I need to take this."

Caden nodded, and Mike walked a few feet away.

"What do you think?"

"I don't know. I'm not liking the feeling I have, Pierre."

"This is not coincidence. First investigating April, and now you see this girl one night and she disappears. Do you think there's a connection?"

"I sure the fuck hope not. I never would have gone out with her."

"You were with April at the fundraiser."

"Fuck." He looked at Caden, who was talking to one of the detectives.

"Did you call her?"

"I will now. We'll figure this out. I'm sending people. They'll be there any minute. You stay clear and tell them you'll give them any info they need, but they know what to do."

"This isn't good."

"We'll handle it, and we'll find Katie."

* * * *

April was finishing up in the meeting upstairs in a private room. She got together with a few business people, all working undercover roles, when a call had come into the fake agency requesting information on what exactly the company did. The person was interested in finding out more information on April Marris, so they connected the person to Julio York, who was really Pierre.

As she walked down the hallway, he spoke to her on her cell phone. She came toward the lobby and bar, stopping to speak with him as she took in the people around the place. She was used to casing out a room when she entered it, and immediately her eyes glanced past two men sitting on chairs looking like they were reading the paper. They had tan complexions, and the one guy looked at her and then quickly looked away. A given that he was waiting to catch a glimpse of her. The other one now put down the paper and played with his cell phone. He was taking her picture. She turned. "I got company."

"What?"

"Yup, two o'clock by the main doors in the lobby. You got people here?"

"Sure do. Just go about your business, April."

"Now why would I do that when we could work on identifying who is doing the snooping?" She smiled and then headed right toward them.

"May not be smart. Katie disappeared. The investigators were on the scene, and they say she was taken. Mike is pissed."

"What?" She stopped short and then had to remind herself that she was trying to get a good look at these two men. "Talk to me. Tell me what's going on and why you're so upset. I mean, I warned you that the guy was a jerk before you went out for dinner with him," she said loudly.

"Jesus, April, I don't know what we're dealing with."

"I'll help with that. Men can be such jerks. Where are all the good men?" She then caught the one guy's eye and looked him over, memorized his face, and gave a soft smile before shyly turning away.

"Watch your ass. You're not even carrying."

"I'll take care of this. Camera's on them, and tell me when you get names. Who is in charge of the other situation?" she asked.

"Caden was on scene and investigators Mike knows. Some of the locals who don't know Mike or who he is are pushing his involvement in her abduction."

"What?"

"Yeah, could turn into a mess."

"Didn't you make calls?"

"We don't know if she's dead or alive. We're handling it."

"Crap."

"I know. Please watch your ass. I've got cameras on you now. Backup nearby."

"Keep them away. Let's see what we're dealing with." She ended the call and then walked by the bar in the lounge area. She took a seat at a high-top table and placed her bag on the chair. She put her cell phone into her bag and pulled out a notepad. She wrote some things down when a bartender walked over. She immediately saw the two men. One went to the left to sit at a tall table, one went to the bar, and she wondered what they were up to.

"Can I get you something to drink?" the waiter asked.

"Definitely. It's been a long day. I'll take a martini shaken, not stirred, two olives, Ketel One please," she said. He nodded.

"Right away, miss." He walked away. He just so happened to walk right next to the guy at the bar and gave the order to the bartender. She watched him make the drink but knew cameras were on him, so if he did something like drugged the drink or something, she would be informed. The waiter returned, and as she thanked him, she began to play her role. She was here on business, but if there was a connection to the overseas case and Rosen and if Katie was taken because of Mike, then she needed to figure out who these men were. She fell right into her role. She reached for the glass, took a small sip, swallowed and then exhaled. She leaned back into the chair and stared at the glass. That was when she noticed another man enter the lounge. She looked back down at the notebook and reached for the pen. She kept the book half on the table and half on her lap and started to write things down. "Call Nate about the investment and contract," "add additional bonus to the deal for Dennis," and a bunch of other bullshit.

"Excuse me." She heard the voice. An accent, not sure from where, and she locked onto deep brown eyes and a rather attractive man. He had a tan complexion, but she wouldn't say it was natural. Definitely from being in the sun.

She raised one eyebrow up at him, and he stared at her, right into her eyes. "I'm sorry, uhm, my English is a little rusty." He sounded Middle Eastern.

"Where are you from?" she asked.

"Turkey," he replied.

"Oh, your accent sounds different, but then again, I've never been to Turkey. What is it you needed?"

"I saw you sitting here alone, enjoying a martini and looking like you had a long day. I did, too. Could I join you?" he asked.

"Uhmm." She pretended shyness, and he raised his hands up.

"I swear I will be a gentleman. I don't like to drink alone."

"I'm only having one. I have another full day of work tomorrow and more to do tonight online." She motioned with her hand for him to sit. "Are you here on business…?" she asked him as he smiled and took the seat.

"Tyler," he said and it was so wrong. You would think the guy would have had a fake name ready if he was going to try and get some info on someone.

"Nice to meet you, Tyler. I'm April," she said, knowing that he would already know her name.

They shook hands, but he brought her hand to his lips and kissed the top. "Very beautiful name, and I must say, your eyes are stunning." He released her hand. "Never have I seen before such beauty."

"Thank you, Tyler. So what business are you here for?" She took another sip of her martini. The bartender brought over a martini for him, too.

"I followed your lead and ordered one on the way in."

No, you didn't. Your buddy by the bar did. Amateur.

She smiled.

"To not drinking alone," he said. She raised her glass, and they tapped glasses.

"So, I am into computer software devices. My partners and I have created our own software, and we continue to expand our line. I'm actually looking for investment firms to represent us. I have an appointment with CLR tomorrow."

"Ahh, I know of them. They are a reputable company. They also help with financial aspects of businesses and banking. Market analysis and cost-effective investments."

He squinted at her. "Don't tell me you work for CLR."

"No, I work for Advance Core, TRC. We're a little smaller but very close-knit and work personally with our clients. Like a family." She took a sip of her martini.

"Interesting. How long have you been with them?" he asked.

"Four years… Well, actually I'll be celebrating five in about three months. It's been great."

"What exactly do you do for them?" he asked and took a sip from his glass and stared at her. She noticed through her peripheral vision that the guy by the bar was turned toward the doorway, and the one in the corner faced them and had that cell phone on her. She wondered if he was zooming in to get a better picture. She screwed with him and shifted to the side, making Tyler block her from the phone.

"Well, investments, contracts, banking, and things. Basically, let's say a client has a product or a business that they are expanding or looking for financial assistance. We can help. Also, if they are negotiating with a buyer, like for patent or to sell off a product or idea for profit, then we help to negotiate terms. We handle a variety of businesses and products, but are selective when it comes to exactly what."

"Selective? How so?" he asked, taking another sip of his martini.

"Well, to be honest, they interview any potential clients, learn what they are looking for, and decide if they are a good fit for TRC. I don't really get involved with that. My bosses know me and the work I do, so I have been fortunate enough to deal with great clients over the years. So how about you? Have you been searching for representation for your computer software long?" she asked him, and he stared at her.

"You're stunning, April, and you sound very intelligent and professional. Maybe I should cancel my appointment with CLR and check out your company more thoroughly." He licked his lips as he eyed over her breasts.

"That's completely up to you. I could give you a number for a contact, but that's all. I honestly wouldn't cancel your appointment. Meet with someone from CLR. Get an idea of how they make you feel and what they think of your software and your vision. Then make one for TRC and see how you feel with them. You'll get a gut instinct on it," she said, and then he gave a nod and a small smile.

"Dinner? You and I and we can talk more?"

"I don't think so. I don't accept dinner dates from men I don't know. Plus, I'll be eating in this evening. I have a heavy workload, and then I'm hoping to close out a deal in the a.m. Thank you anyway," she said to him. He looked a little pissed at her decline.

"In my country when a man asks a beautiful woman to dinner, she complies." His expression grew firm, giving her the creeps.

She took a sip from her martini and held his gaze. "This isn't Turkey, Tyler," she replied, and he smirked and nodded.

"Hmmm, you are quite the beauty, April, and witty, as well. I'll leave you to finish up your drink and get back to work. Thank you for the information."

"Good luck with your appointment."

"I hope to see you again," he said.

"You never know." She watched him go. She took another sip of the martini then watched the other two men get up and walk out a minute later. She finished off the martini, taking her time—she could use the bit of alcohol—then she gathered her things, paid the waiter, and headed out of the lounge. She glanced around the place and was surprised that the one guy who sat at the bar was still there. She stifled a yawn, gave a small smile to a couple walking by, and adjusted the strap of her bag onto her shoulder. She headed toward the elevator and heard her phone go off. The elevator doors opened, and she went to her room, being sure to look around first before opening the door. Once she was inside, she did a sweep of the place, checking all the closets and the bedrooms. The place was huge, and then she plopped onto the couch. She looked at her phone.

Still working?

It was a text message from Simon. Then her cell phone rang. She saw it was Pierre.

"Hello?"

"Well, that was definitely interesting. I have men running their faces through the system. The one guy who came over to talk to you, got into a limo when he left. I got someone on it, license plate coming up as a private agency."

"Well, he lied, said his name was Tyler." She snickered. "He had an accent, Middle Eastern, but claimed to come from Turkey."

"Turkey?"

"Yeah, and there was a marking on his wrist. I only caught a glimpse of it and no idea what it is of, but it was a tattoo. He was definitely fishing. Did his homework though and said he had a meeting with CLR. I told him about TRC, so keep everyone abreast of the situation and a possible inquiry."

"He would definitely be asking for you. The man was eating you up with his eyes."

"Yeah, well, when he asked me to join him for dinner, I told him I don't go to dinner with men I just met, and added that I needed to work. He had an arrogance about him, a confidence, you know. Should be interesting to see where that limo goes."

"Well let's keep the role-playing going. The other men were watching, and the one guy was taking pictures of you or recording you. You did well."

"See, nothing to worry about. I just want to know what the hell is going on and who has been trying to find out more about me."

"I'm asking myself the same question, and with this woman Katie disappearing right after Mike was with her, it's disturbing."

"Are you thinking what I am? That if this guy Kerrin is involved, or even Rosen somehow, that they could be growing that sex slave business. The intel we got on those other businessmen pointed to drugs, partying, prostitution, and weapons. I pray they didn't take Katie to lure Mike in and then take him out."

"I was thinking the same thing. Mike is pretty upset."

"I'll call him."

"How would you know what was happening?"

"I'm going to text Amelia about our lesson for Wednesday morning. I'll ask if all is well, and then she'll call me, fill me in, and there ya go."

"Good idea. Okay, we'll talk tomorrow. Have a good night."

"You too."

She ended the call and texted Amelia. Her response was right on, and then the phone rang. April answered it, and Amelia filled her in on the situation.

"I need to call Mike. He's probably so upset."

"He's with Zayn and Vince, plus the other guys. They're working on trying to find Katie and using their resources."

"Good. Those men all know a lot of people. I'll be back soon. Either Monday night or Tuesday morning. Depends on this deal."

"Okay. Have a safe trip."

"Thanks."

She then texted Simon. *Finishing up now. Need to make a call then I will text.*

* * * *

Mike was standing by the bar with all the guys including Simon, Caden, Aqua, Zayn, Thermo, Selasi, Mike Stelling, and his brothers, Phantom and Turner, who had just ventured out for the first time since nearly getting killed. Mike didn't want to bring anyone down and was debating about leaving and trying to go back to the department, but he knew they would all talk him out of it. Caden and Vince said to let the detectives and agents handle things. He was really worried sick thinking that he caused Katie to be taken.

His cell phone rang, and he glanced at the caller ID. Caden and Zayn looked at him. "It's April," he said and saw the expressions on the guys' faces. Simon just said she texted him back. They had been worried about her, and so was Mike.

"Hey, April."

"Hey, yourself. I heard about Katie. Amelia told me. How are you doing?"

"Shitty," he said and then walked over to the wall away from everyone.

"How are you? You're being careful, and keeping your head on a swivel?"

"Of course, and I have extra eyes on me."

"Anything pop up on the inquiries on you yet?"

"No, but I did get a visit from a few guys who we're keeping on the radar."

"What?" he asked, filled with concern. He saw that Caden was watching him and squinting. He gave him a nod and a small smile, indicating that everything was okay and then he whispered into the phone.

"You watch your ass. What the hell happened?"

"Calm down, I handled it. Played my role well. Three men, one approached me at the bar. Claimed to be from Turkey, but he had a Middle Eastern accent like Syrian or something. Anyway, I drew him in so Pierre and the gang could do their thing."

"Jesus, what happened to staying in the background?"

"I don't know, but between the inquiries, Katie being taken, and these businessmen flying in from all over the place in the next week or so, I would say something is going to happen soon."

"April, you know how these things work. If it's the trading thing that Rosen and Kerrin are into, then she's as good as dead."

"Let's not think that way. Maybe this little skit and getting good images of these guys will help identify them. I'm coming back soon. Maybe tomorrow, otherwise Tuesday evening."

"Good because your men are not happy at all."

"My men?"

"Oh yeah, definitely. Listen, when they let you up for air, I need to talk. I'm going insane here, April. I feel guilty. I more than likely caused this. We were going to meet for lunch. We spent the weekend together, then this happens."

"I understand. No one saw this coming, or would even think anything like this would happen. I'm thinking things through myself. I don't want anything to happen to Caden, Simon, and Aqua. I may need to hold off on dating them."

"Oh boy, they won't take that well."

"They will have to adjust, at least until we get better info on this and see what we're dealing with. I'm going to help Pierre and them with more info tonight. I'll see you in another day."

He said good-bye and then ended the call and walked back over toward them.

"What did April have to say?" Zayn asked.

"She heard about Katie from Amelia. She feels terrible. She's exhausted and working hard, and said we'll get together when she returns."

"When is that, did she say?" Simon asked.

"She wasn't sure last time we spoke to her," Aqua added.

"She mentioned Tuesday or Wednesday. I'm sure she'll call you. When we were talking, someone was beeping in and she had to go," Mike said, but he could tell the three men weren't happy at all.

Then Simon's cell phone rang. He answered it and looked at his brothers. "It's April," he said, and their expressions changed from angry to straight-faced.

* * * *

"Hey, baby. Long day?"

"Oh God, so very long. I can't believe what Amelia told me about Mike. I just called him. I feel terrible. Does Caden know anything?" she asked him.

"He's working on it, but since there was a struggle and there was blood, detectives and some special agents are involved now. It's crazy. How is your hotel? Are you safe? Is security good?" he asked, and she chuckled.

"I'm in a suite with a fully stocked bar, refrigerator, room service, my own personal assistant for any needs or desires I might have, so I think I'm fine." She giggled.

"Every need and desire?" he asked as Caden and Aqua joined him. Their eyes widened, and he covered the mouthpiece and told them about her suite. Caden looked annoyed and rolled his eyes.

"Well, maybe not every need and desire. So how are you guys? The town must be buzzing with concerns. Any leads?"

"None, and people are shaken up because they know Katie from her being a nurse at the hospital. We're hoping these detectives can get something soon. The more hours that pass, the more difficult it is to find someone who has been taken."

"I know. Let's pray she's found safe and sound."

"So, when will you have this deal sealed up?"

"Ahh, the ten-million-dollar question. I don't know. He's being resistant, but this trip was necessary, and I think after the meeting in the morning, I should have a better idea. I made some additional contacts and will be pretty busy for a while when I return. My boss was here, too. He's quite the character, and he shows a bit of favoritism, which leads to more work for me. Anyway, I don't want to bore you with the details. I know you're at Corporal's. How are Caden and Aqua? Is Caden handling this abduction okay, or is the media all over him?"

"I'll put him on. He's doing well, and surprisingly the media isn't harassing him anymore. They got their little clip for the news earlier today. I miss you, baby. Can't wait until you're back."

"I miss you, too."

He handed the phone to Caden. "She's worried about you and handling this abduction," he whispered and handed Caden the phone.

* * * *

Caden took the phone.

"Hey, sweetie, when you coming home?" he asked all serious.

"Soon, Caden. How are you holding up?"

"I'm fine. Don't you worry about me. How is this deal going?"

"Taking forever. I just filled in Simon, so he can tell you. I'm not sure if I'll be back tomorrow night or earlier. Can you take care of Mike please? I'm sure he's going crazy. Even though he just met Katie and things happened over the weekend, he likes her."

"We will, don't you worry. Just can't wait to have you back in our arms."

"Let me say hello to Aqua, and then I'm going back onto the computer before a hot bath and bed."

"You sure security is good there?"

"Yes, Chief, it's safe."

"Okay, talk to you tomorrow. Here's Aqua."

Aqua took the phone from Caden, and Caden listened as he spoke to Simon.

"I miss her. How does she sound to you?"

"Tired and a bit distant, like laying groundwork for more busy things with work and making new contacts, thanks to her boss who is there, too."

"Fuck, I wonder who he is. Think he's hitting on her?" Caden asked, and Simon put on a mean face.

"I expect you back real soon, and we'll be there to greet you then take you to bed. I miss that sexy body, and that firm round ass pressed against my cock," Aqua told her, and Caden and Simon chuckled and shook their heads. Thank goodness no one could hear Aqua. He winked at them and then spoke softly to her. "I expect a call as soon as you know you're leaving and what time that limo will drop you off at your house. We'll be waiting," he said and then talked a little longer before ending the call and handing the phone to Simon.

"Goddamn I miss her," Aqua said and then took his beer from the bar and guzzled it down.

"We do, too. I just want her back here in our arms, safe and sound. The idea that some creep is out there and abducted Katie makes me feel even more protective," Simon said.

"I can't believe we feel like this. I mean, we're fucking Seals, and this woman has us all crazy inside," Simon said.

"This is fucking torture. That's what it is," Aqua stated.

"Well, we better get used to it if she's going to be our woman. She has a career and needs to travel. Next time she's heading overseas, she said," Simon added.

"Don't remind me. Let's just get her back here to Mercy as soon as possible. I'm uneasy not knowing where she is, who is near her, and what guys are hitting on her."

"Aqua, she isn't going to cheat on us. She doesn't even date," Simon replied.

"We don't know what she does or even fully what kind of woman she is. We just know the lust, the attraction is there, and when we're all making love it's fucking incredible. Now we have to find out deeper things."

"Sounds like a plan for when she returns," Simon said then took a slug from his bottle of beer.

"Maybe we'll get around to it, but first things first when she gets home. Straight to bed and maybe we'll let her out by the weekend," Caden told them, and they chuckled then clinked their beer bottles together. Caden couldn't help but to smile. April brought them even closer together than they were before, and on top of that she could be the one woman to make their lives complete. So why was he feeling a bit of trepidation in his gut?

Chapter Seven

"Well, Pierre, one of my teams spotted a redhead being brought from a plane to the jeeps at the air mat in Syria. It has to be that Katie woman who was abducted," Colonel Brothers said to him.

"Son of a bitch, these guys are out for revenge, yet no one went after Mike. I don't get it."

"Well, they could have gone after her because she was with him, and that was it. Or maybe they just had an order for a redhead. These fucking guys are ruthless, though I have to say from past experience she must be a bit important and like they want to keep her alive. Otherwise, she would be with all the other women they abduct and then sell off as sex slaves. It makes me sick, and we can't do a thing about it.'

"That isn't our mission or yours, but it seems to be pointing toward this sex slave business as well as guns and heroin. What I'm afraid of is these inquiries over who April is."

"Could be that they saw her with Mike and then got thrown off when Mike hooked up with the redhead, so they went after her."

"Could be, but then these guys show up and they know April is in the hotel. The guy approaches, and she spotted two others immediately before this guy shows up. They converse, and she gets suspicious. We got his name and had him followed until he got out near the department stores and the limo left. We lost him."

"Nothing came up on the computers?"

"Not yet. I got people working on things. April headed out to the airport. She wanted to get home to help with the case with Mike."

"She should be lying low. Did you tell her about Evan and the connection to those Seals she's seeing?"

"Not yet. I think if I do let her know that they knew Evan and he had been part of their team for a few years that she might break things off. She's fighting things tooth and nail."

"Can't blame her. She could have died out there. When she took out those men and saved my guys and my life, it was incredible."

"Then you guys saved hers and got her medical attention before she bled out."

"Was a miracle all around. I'll keep watch on the redhead. You guys keep doing your intel, and we'll do ours. Something has to give. Some indication that a deal is going to happen and soon," Colonel said, and Pierre agreed. Something had to give soon. They were close, but they had to keep digging.

* * * *

When the car pulled up, she caught sight of the truck and the three large men leaning back against it with the tailgate down. They had a case of beer and several pizza boxes. She smiled at the sight. The limo stopped, and the driver got her bags as the men approached. Simon pulled her into his arms, and she squeezed him tight.

"Missed you so damn much," he said to her.

"I missed you, too," she replied. She pulled back and thanked the driver, and then Simon took her bags. Aqua hugged her next. He kissed her tenderly and ran his hand over her ass and then cupped her breast.

When he released her lips, he growled. "You got my dick so hard, baby. I need you desperately." He nipped her lip. She felt the need, too. She truly missed them.

"Get the pizza and the beer. She looks hungry and tired," Caden ordered, and Aqua gave her a wink and released her. She pulled the strap of her bag onto her shoulder, and Caden looked her over. "Get over here, woman. What are you doing wearing something so sexy and without us with you?" he asked, looking at the slim-fitting business dress in navy blue. She went right to him and hugged him tight. He squeezed her to him and then kissed her neck and inhaled. "Missed you so much."

"Me too," she said, and then they headed toward the front door. She reached into her purse and undid the locks and disarmed the alarm. They entered, and Simon locked the door behind them.

They placed the pizza boxes down on the counter and the beer, too. She slid off her heels and then wiggled her toes. "God, I'm so tired." She exhaled.

"Come sit down and eat something," Simon told her.

"Let me grab some paper plates," she said.

"Point and I'll get them. You sit down," Aqua said, and she smiled and pointed to the closet. He pulled them out, and then they started passing along slices of pizza and handed her a beer.

She took a few bites, then a sip of beer as she watched them eating and drinking. Her pussy clenched, and her nipples hardened. They were so sexy, so big and muscular and all hers. She missed them. Who was she kidding? She wanted them. She dropped the piece of pizza down on the paper plate, wiped her mouth, and then took a sip of beer. She stood up.

"What do you need?" Aqua asked. She stepped between his legs. He dropped the pizza down on the plate, and she slid her palms up his chest.

"You. All three of you," she told him and stood up on tiptoes to reach his lips. He immediately picked her up and kissed her. She straddled his hips, and he carried her to her bedroom. She heard the chairs at the counter scraping and then footsteps following. Aqua released her lips and set her feet down on the floor. A second set of hands unzipped her dress and pressed the material down. Aqua stared at her breasts as they fell from the top. "I need so bad I ache," he said to her. Her dress fell to the rug. Simon pushed her panties down, and then Aqua cupped her breasts. She moaned, but she needed, too. She stepped from her panties and then lowered to her knees, undid Aqua's pants, and shoved them down. As he tried stepping out of them, she licked his cock from balls to tip and then took him into her mouth. She began to suck, and he moaned and gripped her hair.

"Damn, woman," he said, and she felt Simon kneel down behind her, kiss her shoulder, wrap an arm around her waist, and slide fingers into her cunt from behind.

"Spread those thighs, and let me in. Let me see how wet and ready you are for your men," he said, and she moaned and rocked her hips.

Simon gripped her hair, caressed it, and then gave it a tug. Her eyes darted to Caden who was naked and holding his cock in his other hand. She slid her mouth from Aqua's and went to suck Caden's. Back and forth, she took turns sucking each of them when she felt Simon replace fingers with his cock. She jerked forward, her cheek against Caden's cock as he caressed her hair, and Simon thrust into her pussy from behind. She pulled back and went to suck on Aqua's cock. She went back and forth, and then Caden lay down on the bed, legs spread wide and his cock in his hand. His legs were over the edge. She slid her palms along his thighs, and then Simon pulled out, lifted her up, and deposited her onto Caden. She ran her hands up his chest and kissed him as Simon licked her from cunt to asshole back and forth. He slid a finger into her cunt and then one into her ass. She moaned, pulled from Caden's lips, and lifted up. He gripped her hips, and she lowered her pussy to his cock, taking him deep to her womb. They both exhaled. She felt fingers stroking her ass, the bed dip, and now Aqua was naked and holding his cock.

"Together the way it will always be," he said to her. His words fired her up and made her want things and pretend for now that she had a different life and that danger wasn't hiding around a corner nearby. She opened wide and took his cock into her mouth as Caden thrust upward. Caden pinched her nipple and tugged on it. He cupped her breast as he rocked his hips, and she suckled harder, faster, bobbing her head up and down on Aqua's cock. Then she felt Simon replace his fingers with his cock and slide into her asshole. The four of them moaned, and it was on. Like wild needy lovers who had been apart for months and the reunited, they thrust and stroked into one another over and over again. It was like no one wanted to come. They wanted the sensations, the deep connection to last, and it did. The orgasms hit her one after the next, and then finally Aqua came in her mouth. She licked him clean and then moaned and cried out another release. Simon came in her ass, smacked it several times, and then kissed her back as he slid from her body. Caden rolled her to her back, spread her arms above her head, and hammered into her cunt over and over again before he poured his seed into her womb. He hugged her to him and kissed her everywhere he could. "I missed you, sugar. So very much."

"I missed you, too," she whispered, and then they all snuggled on the bed until her stomach began to growl.

"Ready for some more pizza and then back to bed?" Caden asked, stroking her hip and then clenching her chin before kissing her again.

"Bed to sleep. I'm so tired. I didn't sleep well," she admitted.

"Worrying about Mike and Katie?" Simon asked.

"Yes, and missing the three of you." She leaned forward and kissed Caden on the lips then to his chest.

* * * *

Mike headed out of the department. He was exhausted and knew that he needed sleep. As he got into the car and began to drive, his cell phone rang. He answered it, stifling a yawn. "Yeah."

"Where are you?"

"Heading home."

"Don't. We got word that some men who were working for Vince Turbin, and are considered trackers, are in the vicinity, and considering that we still don't have concrete information on those men in New York who spoke to April, we shouldn't take any chances," Pierre told him.

"What do you suggest I do? Head back to the department?"

"Head out of town. Go to the hotel. I've got a team there on standby."

Mike gripped the steering wheel, and as he came to the red light and turned on his blinker, he saw the truck heading straight toward him.

"Too late. They found me."

"What?" Pierre yelled. Mike stepped on the gas to make the turn, and the truck rammed into him. He lost complete control of the vehicle, slammed his head forward, his body crushed from the metal, and his car flipped over. It happened so quickly. The crashing sound, the rev of the engine, his body slamming forward, backward, then side to side as the car flipped and ended upside down. Then came the truck again slamming into it. He was going to die. Son of a bitch. He lost his focus, and they won. Katie would die if she weren't dead already.

* * * *

"What the fuck do you mean a truck slammed into him? Is he dead?" Aqua asked Caden as he joined him in the kitchen. Caden was on the phone. He had missed several calls and messages from the department and from Zayn and Watson. He was on the phone with Watson now.

"Something fucking strange is going on here. First Katie and then Mike. Do you think he was involved with something, a case or whatever, and these men are out for revenge?" Zayn asked.

"I'm thinking the same thing, but first things first, we have to tell April. She'll be so upset. She's showering right now, and we were getting ready to make some breakfast. She'll want to get to the hospital," Caden said and looked at Aqua. Simon entered the room, hair still wet from his shower with April, and he was smiling. Caden felt his chest tighten. Simon stopped short.

"What?" he asked.

Caden spoke into the phone.

"We'll get April, and we'll meet you at the hospital." He ended the call.

"Hospital? Who?" Simon asked.

"Mike. Someone tried to kill him early this morning. They slammed into his car with a large box truck. He's alive," Caden told him then heard his cell phone go off. He squinted at what he read.

"What? What does it say?" Aqua asked.

"From Zayn. He said federal agents are there, took over security, and stated that Mike is dead."

"What?" April asked, entering the kitchen, looking gorgeous and now stunned.

Simon pulled her into his arms. "It's Mike, baby. He was in a car accident last night."

"No, no, tell me he isn't dead," she said as tears filled her eyes.

"Zayn said he's alive, but that federal agents got there, took over, and now texted. They are saying Mike is dead."

"What? Oh God, we need to go there," she said, pulling from his arms.

"Wait." Simon grabbed her hand. Caden took in the sight of her. The tight hip-hugging capris in cream and the tank top in a light green along with her heeled sandals, she looked sexy and classy. His heart hammered inside of his chest.

"Maybe you shouldn't go there. Maybe it's too dangerous. We don't know what Mike is involved in, and we don't want you in any danger," he said.

She squinted and then recovered. "He's my friend. How could I not go there to find out what the hell happened? What could possibly be going on? He's done work for the federal government. Technically he's an agent but working out of the state police barracks. It would be normal for the feds to show up, wouldn't it be?"

Caden looked at her. "He could be involved with something bad. Like maybe whomever tried to kill him went after Katie to get to him, to lure him in," Caden said, and she covered her mouth with her hand and then put her hand down.

"So you think I shouldn't go to the hospital to see my friend who may die if he hasn't already?" she asked. Caden heard the anger in her voice. Simon wrapped his arm around her waist.

"We'll go with you. They may not even let you near him to see him," Simon told her and hugged her from behind. She turned her head to look up at him. Caden thought she looked so beautiful, feminine, and sweet. He didn't want her exposed to this shit, to any danger. Had questions about how she even knew Mike and became friends, but now wasn't the time to ask or to come across as jealous.

"Let's eat something and go," Caden said.

She nodded, and Simon released her. "I have a bunch of things in the refrigerator," she said and went toward it.

"I'll fix us some eggs. You point out where everything is," Aqua said to her.

"We'll do it together," she said and caressed Aqua's arm. He winked at her and they prepared breakfast, but Caden felt that ache in his gut clench a little deeper.

* * * *

"What do you mean he's alive?" Kulta asked.

"The fucking guy didn't die. We rammed the shit out of him. The car flipped over and the hood was caved in. Pretty certain he was dead, but we couldn't finish him off with a bullet. You said not to, and then there were cars coming and we needed to get the fuck out of there."

"Shit. Okay, you got rid of the truck. Doesn't matter if the cops find it. I want you to meet up with the others. There's been a change of plans. I got my orders, and I'm going to need several men just in case."

"Okay, we'll be at the location waiting by the phone."

"Good. I'll be in touch."

Kulta ended the call and then licked his lips. He looked at the pictures he had spread out on the table in the hotel. He sent them along to the team of men. This would be an easy snag, but considering the many cops and agents around this fucking town, he wasn't taking chances. No way was he going to piss off Gorbin and Fulta. He stared at his phone. When they said to move in and do the job, he would be ready.

Chapter Eight

April was fuming mad. It was difficult to not show that anger and to not react. To not answer her cell phone and get updates from Pierre. When they got to the hospital, it was intense to say the least. Security was high on the floor Mike was on. He was in the ICU, and they were told it was touch and go. She didn't recognize any of the agents, and none of them seemed to look at her as if they knew her. They shouldn't. Not many people knew who she was, including her men. She felt so guilty right now. She wanted to share with them who she was, but with this recent attack on Mike, Katie being abducted, and those men watching her and the one approaching in New York, she was on edge. They still didn't know if she was being looked at because of Mike and her relationship to him just like Katie.

Her last text to Pierre was her plan to draw them in. To be seen here, distraught, over Mike's accident. With her men in tow, it could confuse those who were hunting Mike and causing him this pain. It could also make her men targets. This had to end. She hoped the recent information she sent Pierre on the plane was helping in some way.

"She's the closest thing to family he has. Let her see him," Caden said to one of the federal agents. They talked back and forth, and she waited. They let her in, and the sight of Mike looking pretty much dead tore at her heart. It was easy to show her emotions. To let the tears flow. He looked like hell. Tubes everywhere, bandages, bruises, cuts, swollen eyes, damaged cheek, and a slew of injuries that would lead him into several surgeries to save his life. She felt the hands go to her hips, and Caden pressed his body to hers. "He'll pull through," he said to her. She reached out, not knowing where to touch he was such a mess. She went to his hand and stroked the top then leaned closer.

"I'm here, Mike. Keep fighting. You got this, Mike. You got this," she said to him then lowered down and kissed his hand.

The nurses ushered them out pretty quickly.

April needed to get on the phone with Pierre and see what the plans were. She was antsy as the men walked with her outside and then toward the truck.

"Don't you have work today?" she asked Caden.

"I do, but I took off to be with you."

"Caden, I'm fine. I feel better that I got to see him." She swallowed hard. Aqua pulled her next to him in the back seat of the truck. He kept his hand over her thigh as Caden and Simon got into the front of the truck.

"We missed you being away for a couple of days. Figured we could spend the day together," Caden told her.

"I'd like that. I do have a few things to just check on with emails and stuff," she replied, thinking she could probably go into the bedroom or someplace to make a few calls.

"Do what you need to do. We'll hang out while you do it." Simon spoke up. She leaned her head against Aqua. She felt conflicted. She went and fell in love with these men. She wasn't going to put them into any danger. She didn't care about anything else but their safety. They had gone through so much in their lives, in their careers. They could die if these men who went after Mike went after her. She wasn't going to let that happen.

* * * *

"April wants protection for Caden, Simon, and Aqua," Pierre said to Colonel Brothers.

"She does realize that they're Seals?"

"She's in love with them. She's concerned and rightfully so. The intel we have is pointing at Syrians that came to the hotel to visit. I'm trying to get confirmation on who they work for. All avenues seem to be leading to Kerrin Bulla."

"Son of a bitch. Do you think he knows she's the one who killed Turbin, the one who help to kill those men on the boat in Cypress?"

"I sure the fuck hope not. It doesn't make sense. Going after Katie, who we got nothing on, and then Mike."

"Revenge?"

"Could be, but no one knows that April is basically a spy. Then of course the recent info she got points to some big business meeting happening in the next few days somewhere in Syria. You said there were women being transported and that someone saw a redhead that matched Katie's description? Could they be bringing the women in for these businessmen?" Pierre asked.

"I wouldn't doubt it. I just got some intel from my men there in Syria. They said food is being ordered, that a woman is in charge of entertainment for the men. There's some chatter about special orders," Colonel Brothers told him.

"Damn, this could be about the business those men want to push. Guns, women, drugs, and setting up cells for terrorist attacks. They get the money backings from these businessmen, maybe keep them happy with women and drugs, and then Rosen and Kerrin do their thing."

"Have you told April about Evan's relationship with Caden, Simon, and Aqua? He was part of their team at one point. Then he was out for a time with injury and got put with that other unit temporarily."

"No, I didn't. Right now if I did then she would definitely cut them off and insist we really cover them. Maybe even take them into protective holding." Colonel Brothers laughed.

"Holy shit, she does love them. Never thought I would see the day that sexy blonde let someone into her heart. She's fierce."

"Yeah, but against odds like these and a multitude of men, while also trying to keep her men safe and her friends safe, she could be over her head."

"Let's hope not. Try to get names to those men who saw her at the hotel. I'll do the same on my end."

* * * *

Watson, Dell, and Fogerty were dropping off Amelia for an hour to train with April. Caden, Simon, and Aqua were there too and talking to them.

"Come back in an hour or so," April said.

"How about we do lunch? Want to go meet up someplace when they're done?" Watson asked.

"I could do that. I'm working, but get a lunch anyway," Caden said and squeezed April's shoulders then kissed her neck.

He was feeling uneasy. He didn't like leaving her, and he worried about her constantly. Caden was caught between being a man, a Seal, and letting this sexy bombshell of theirs turn him into a vulnerable guy. He was thinking about her all the time, and so were Simon and Aqua. In fact, Simon mentioned where the relationship was going and that maybe they should ask her to move in with them. Then of course Aqua pointed out that she wouldn't leave her place for theirs, and that got them talking about her income, and how well off she was. She didn't really need them to take care of her financially. It was a roller coaster of emotions.

"We could grab some things at the store and come back and get things started," Aqua suggested.

"We'll go too and come back here and set things up while the ladies enjoy their training," Dell said.

"Well, give us a little more than an hour them. Bring back some clothes for Amelia. We can go swimming like we usually do and then hang out by the pool," April said.

"Sounds like a plan," Simon replied, and they all agreed.

"You good with that, April?" Fogerty asked, and she gave a thumbs-up and winked. Caden felt a twinge of something, but then

April gave him a kiss good-bye then Aqua and Simon too before she and Amelia headed to the training room April had set up. Totally state-of-the-art and she claimed most of it was for show. One look at her body in the sports bra, short tank top, and spandex shorts and he knew she was bluffing. His gut clenched again, but then they all headed out and he went back to work.

* * * *

April and Amelia were working out.

"So things are going really well with the chief and his brothers?" Amelia asked.

"Definitely very well."

"So awesome. They seem very serious. Do they relax any, or are the three of them always in Seal mode?" Amelia asked.

April chuckled. "They relax a bit, but I know what you mean. You probably can see more because your men are Special Forces. Those guys can be just as intense."

"I suppose most soldiers are, and then add in the elite ones and definitely they have a hard time relaxing."

She was showing her some moves when April caught sight of movement through the windows outside. It was quick, and so was her reaction as one man in black, holding a gun, approached. She grabbed Amelia. Amelia screamed. The door burst open. April pressed the wall, and it opened. "Get in there. It will lock. Air will flow. Pick up the phone immediately."

"April, what's going on?" Amelia screamed as April shoved her inside and slammed the fake wall, a door and special panic room, closed. She knew that Amelia was safe, but now she had these guys to deal with.

"Come with us. No trouble. Let's go," the one guy yelled to her as the other one went to try and open the wall. He wouldn't be able to.

"I don't think so," she said and went to run to the right. The guy reached out to grab her, and she throat punched him and took him down. The other one came at her. She disarmed him, took his gun, when the door opened again and others were going to come in. She raced toward them, shooting the gun, hitting one, two, and then a third in the head. She ran out, needing to get to the house, to her weapons, and waste time until the cavalry arrived. If Amelia kept her head together, she should have picked up the phone by now, and Pierre would be sending in men. She ran to the house and felt the sting to her neck. She stopped, placed her hand on her neck, and felt the dart. "Poison." Her initial thought was to run inside, but then she feared for her men and for Amelia's. They would be coming back soon. This had to end. She heard their voices and then felt the arm around her waist and the gun being pulled from her hand. She started to sink to the ground, and he picked her up. He spoke in Syrian as an SUV sped up the driveway. They pulled her inside, and she knew she may never see her men again. They were safe though, and so was Amelia. That's what mattered first.

* * * *

"Men in black. April is in trouble. She shoved me into this room in the wall in the gym. Oh God, they had guns. I hear gunfire. They're going to kill her. Help us."

"Calm down, Amelia. I have men on the way. You hang tight. How many men?"

"I don't know. One outside and then there were others coming into the room. I heard gunfire. She could be shot and dead right now."

"I need you to calm down. She put you in there to protect you. Nothing can penetrate that wall. We'll get to you shortly."

"Oh my God. Oh my God, what is going on?"

* * * *

Caden sped up the road. There were so many cars, black SUVs with tinted windows, agents walking around. He didn't know what the fuck was happening.

Then he saw his brothers, Zayn, Watson, and Dell, and a few other men in suits. He got out of the police truck.

"What the hell happened?" he demanded to know.

"It's a fucking mess. There are several dead bodies, two men out cold inside the training room, and April is missing," Simon told him.

"Dead bodies? What the fuck is going on?"

"April and Amelia were training, and they saw a guy in black outside approaching," Zayn said as he held Amelia close.

Amelia started talking. "She saved me. She shoved me into this secret space in the wall in the gym. There was a phone on the wall. She said to pick it up and someone would answer. Then I heard gunshots, and she saved me, Caden. She could have gone in there with me, but the men were coming at her and she closed the door and they took her."

His head was spinning as Aqua explained about the belief that April took out five men and disarmed and knocked out two more. They were already being taken in by federal agents.

"Federal agents? How the fuck does April know federal agents and have a room like that in the gym?" he asked.

He looked at his brothers and his friends.

"Some serious shit is going on here," Zayn said to him.

"Excuse me." They heard a voice and turned to see some tall guy in a black suit approach. The other agents and people on scene moved out of the way.

"I'm Special Agent Pierre Franks. If the three of you will follow me inside, we can talk about the situation."

Caden looked at Zayn, Dell, and Fogerty.

"I need to keep this small. April doesn't want you involved in any way, and that means friends included," he said to them. "Follow me," Pierre told them.

"Go ahead, you need answers," Fogerty told them, and Caden, Simon, and Aqua walked into April's house with Special Agent Franks.

They were stunned as Pierre explained who April really was, and about the case and connections to Frank and even Amelia's rescue and her killing Turbin.

"Holy shit, that was April?" Aqua asked and ran his hand over his jaw.

"She took a great risk taking him out. She's been taking a lot of risks trying to protect not only you and her friends, but others like Mike and other military personnel. I'll explain as much as I can quickly, as you can imagine we have people tracking the men that took April to the airport."

"Airport? Where the fuck to? What do they want with her?" Simon asked.

"Our intel, prior to her killing those men outside, was that they thought she was important to Mike. That's why Katie was taken. She's been seen being transported to the same location we think these men took April. Since only the one person who took her now realizes her capabilities, it won't be long before they figure out who she is, and that she isn't just capable of shooting a gun and being a martial arts expert. They find out she's a spy, a special agent, and they link her to Cypress, then they could kill her on the spot," Pierre said.

"Fuck." Simon exhaled.

"Cypress? What happened in Cypress?" Caden asked.

Pierre exhaled and then looked away and then back at them.

"She's in love with you guys. After today, the three of you were going to be under total protection. Her orders were that if you got in the way, then you would be taken to a special protection facility."

"What?" Caden asked and paced.

"She does know that we're Navy Seals?" Simon asked. Now he was pissed off.

"She knows everything about you, and that's why she didn't want you to get hurt. Listen, I don't have time for all the details. She was protecting you. She knows about why you retired, Caden. About the ambush and you nearly dying. She knows why Simon and Aqua have been doing few jobs in between. She knew Evan, as well."

"What?" the three of them asked at the same time. Caden felt the emotions, the anger and confusion. Evan was like a brother to them. He was killed in a mission working for their commander, Colonel Brothers. He should have been assigned with them, but it was his first full mission back after injury and he knew the job well. It was a clusterfuck of an operation. One agent survived, but not before killing terrorists and helping to save the Seals who were heading into a trap. His eyes widened.

"She was the agent? The one who saved Colonel Brothers and the other Seals?"

"What?" Simon asked, not putting things together so quickly.

Pierre nodded. "Evan and April were seeing one another for a short period of time."

From there Pierre gave them a little more information about April's life, her career, and her capabilities.

"We want in on this," Simon said.

"No can do."

"Bullshit. You know all about us and what we can handle," Aqua said.

"It isn't my call, and it's not what April wanted."

"She was too worried about us getting hurt and about Evan and what happened to him. She will need us if these men are as bad as you say. Let us in. Give us the information," Simon demanded.

Pierre shook his head. "I made a promise."

Caden growled and slammed his hand down on the table.

"This is insane!" he roared.

Pierre stared at them. "I made a promise to not let you get involved. That I wouldn't share the information I have with any of you. Perhaps Colonel Brothers feels differently," he said and then walked out of the kitchen.

"Caden?" Aqua said, and Caden nodded, pulled out his cell phone. It rang once.

"Thought I would hear from you sooner," Colonel Brothers said.

"We want in. NO fucking bullshit," he stated.

"Figured as much. That woman of yours is super special and capable. They drugged her, otherwise there would be two more dead bodies there."

"You know her well then."

"Very. We've worked together over the years trying to take down these men who more than likely have her. They're responsible for many agents' and soldiers' deaths, and Evan's, too."

"We heard. We want in, so tell us where to meet you and how to get updated quickly."

"Sit tight. I'll send someone for you. Don't worry about gear. The next several hours, you'll be overloaded with information and intel, then I'll decide your role and how close you'll be to the action. April is going to be pissed off."

"Well, she'll have to deal with it. We're pretty pissed off, too."

* * * *

"I have a surprise for you, Rosen."

Rosen looked at Victoria as she slid her palm along his shoulders. She wore a black pantsuit and was done up for this evening's dinner event. The party already started, the men were choosing their women, and special orders were being presented all around them. He leaned back. "I told you not to worry about me. I have very particular tastes." He ran his finger along the rim of his glass.

"I know you do. I know you will be quite pleased. Indulge me, and when the meeting is done, arrangements made, and everyone is beginning to enjoy themselves fully, go to your room, the special quarters I specifically chose for you, and enjoy the treat."

He exhaled in annoyance. Then Kerrin Bulla arrived and joined them.

"Ahh, Victoria, it's always a pleasure seeing you."

"As it is to see you, Kerrin. I hope you enjoy the entertainment. Now I'll leave you to your business," Victoria said and walked away with two of her guards, Gorbin and Fulta.

"I take it your delivery went well?" Rosen said to Kerrin, joining him at the bar.

"The businessmen were impressed. The shipment is on its way to Kuwait, and we, my friend, have the monetary backing of seven very wealthy businessmen. I would say things went according to plan," Kerrin replied.

"That isn't what I heard," Rosen said to him.

"What do you mean?"

Roses took a sip from his drink and then placed it down. He narrowed his eyes at Kerrin. "Did you seriously think that I wouldn't find out about the hit? About your need to take out the agent you think was involved in the Cypress incident? I said to leave that warehouse alone, and you didn't listen."

"It went smoothly. Those guns were important, and getting a little revenge on that fucking agent is priceless."

"You think so, Kerrin?"

"I know so, and I'll get even more pleasure when I fuck the redhead he bedded and then slit her fucking throat. The only bad thing is he didn't die, but I hear he's bound to."

"You're a fool. You've jeopardized my operation, my business dealings. So, you know, I've pulled out my share and covered my tracks. Revenge sought can be the demise of many successful men."

Kerrin smirked. "I know the agent who survived Cypress and killed those men. Your men and mine, and rescued the other Seals, giving them opportunity to capture others and take my weapons."

Rosen squinted at him.

"Ahh, caught your interest now, even though you don't seek revenge."

"Go on."

"You won't believe it."

"Try me."

"It's a woman. We didn't realize until my little desire to seek revenge caught sight of her with Mike Waters. A blonde beauty with green eyes and capabilities."

Rosen was completely interested. Kerrin smiled. "I did not mean to go behind your back, but you've been so distant lately. Since losing Evette, your little pet." Rosen ground his teeth. "I mean no disrespect. When Victoria figured things out with Gorbin and Fulta, and this woman killed several of our good men when they tried to take her, we dug deeper and the truth was revealed. She was the agent on the boat. The one Bo and Kona double-crossed. She was also responsible for killing Turbin. She's a spy of sorts. Very capable. Can shoot, fight, and who else knows what. A perfect match for you, and waiting in your room for you to do as you like. Our gift to you, Rosen, and all you've done for Victoria and I," he said, shocking Rosen.

"Go ahead. The deals are done. Weapons are being moved as we speak, drugs delivered, and a party in the works. This is a night to celebrate, and for dessert, I get the little redhead," Kerrin said and stuck out his tongue and wiggled it before he chuckled, took his glass, and walked away.

Rosen downed the rest of his drink. This spy, this blonde, sounded amazing. She would have a fight in her, and that was something he liked in his slaves. They seemed to be able to handle the beatings accordingly.

He stood up and locked gazes with Victoria who was rubbing some guy's shoulders. He nodded, and she gave a wink and a smile then lipped the word "enjoy."

* * * *

Aqua, Caden, and Simon moved in sync with the other Seal teams and Special Forces guys. They stopped several shipments from reaching their destinations. Time was running out though. They were helping to do these separate hits and stop weapons and ammunition from getting into the hands of terrorist cells. Their minds were on April though and where she was being held. So as they stood in position and got info from intel, they grew more and more impatient.

"We got a location on Katie, but nothing on April," Colonel Brothers told them.

"Fuck, do you think she's even here?" Aqua asked.

"She was seen being carried in days ago. We have four teams with us. Everyone has their objective and targets. We've intercepted all deliveries of illegal weapons, and have captured or killed dozens of these pieces of shit. We will have complete success with this. Believe me, April is resourceful."

"She's also tranquilized," Simon stated.

"She's well trained, as you gathered from what was shared with you. That information wasn't everything," he told them, and Caden clenched his teeth. Their woman was a fucking spy. Holy fucking shit, it seemed she was more capable then even they were. She even used her capabilities and connections to rescue Amelia and take out Turbin. He would never forget that day. The way she gave the thumbs-up dressed like a guy in a disguise obviously. She knew who they were. She even escaped through the elevator shaft, and no one saw a thing. No cameras, nothing. She was pro and then some. Why did that make him feel proud besides jealous? He took a deep breath and released it then looked at his brothers.

"We knew she was special the moment we laid eyes on her. She fucking knew Evan," Aqua said to them.

"It was meant to be, and if he hadn't been killed, he would be sharing her with us. Let's focus on that, and getting her back safe and sound," Caden said. Suddenly, explosions began to go off, and gunfire erupted around the building.

"What the fuck?" one of the men said aloud.

"April. I told you she's resourceful. Let's move in."

* * * *

April waited until the stupid guards left the room. She was dressed in some sort of sheer garb and smelled like sweet perfume that was making her gag. They were stupid enough to leave her hands untied, and the moment the door opened and she peeked her eyes, open she saw that it was all clear. One guard outside of the door that she knew of, no one in the room. She heard them speaking about women being delivered and the redhead. It had to be Katie. She was ready to go find her and take out who she could, when the guard mentioned that Rosen was coming. Then the woman, Victoria, arrived. She touched her, and it was creepy, but April didn't make a sound or move. She played possum well. If the bitch fondled her any more, she would take her out. She didn't have to, though. And she knew that her research and the info she sent Pierre just hours before the attack at her home meant she was on the right track. Pierre and the team, hopefully Colonel Brothers, would have the information on Victoria. The bitch ran an illegal sex slave business. She had men all over the world abducting women to provide a catered menu to a man's precise needs and wants. It was disturbing, and even worse was how those women were disposed of for an additional payment. It made April sick, and even though she could have escaped from the men who took her, she knew this case needed to be finished. That Pierre and the Colonel were on top of things and would get here to assist. Their players, the businessmen, and this woman Victoria would all go down.

What she didn't want to think about were Caden, Simon, and Aqua. When they found out who she really was, they more than likely would hate her for lying to them and keeping her identity secret. Her relationship with them would be done. That was her life. These were the things she gave up on as a spy. She could never have true love and a commitment. Her time with her men would be nothing but a memory.

She cleared her head and focused on her objective, and hoped that the colonel had arrived. She slid off the bed. Her muscles were a little funny, but her immunity to the tranquilizers took special skills. She looked around the room. Then she headed to the door. It was about to get real.

She slowly pulled the door open, and there was the guard. She pulled him back and broke his neck. Quickly she grabbed his weapon, the ammo, and the knife. Her attire wasn't exactly combat ready, but she would make do. First she needed a distraction so she could get to Katie.

As she moved along the hallways, other guards appeared. One after the next, she took them out quietly and then got to the staircase. She looked out the window and saw the barrels of what she hoped was gasoline or something flammable below. She bent down, yanked a grenade from the guard's utility belt, then grabbed another one. She pulled the ring, one, two, and then tossed them onto the barrels. She bent down low, covered her head, and the explosions rocked the building.

She took a deep breath as she heard yelling and then men running past the staircase. Katie was in the room down the hallway. She headed that way. When the bullets whizzed by her head, she ducked and turned and took out two guards then continued along the path. She got to the door, saw the guard, and took him out. She got the door open, and there was a man, Kerrin Bulla, about to rape Katie.

"Get away from her!" she yelled. He turned, and she shot him. He went down, and Katie lay there unconscious. "Shit," she said aloud. How the hell was she going to get her out of here? Then April heard the gunshots, then yelling and more shots coming closer. She prayed it was Colonel Brothers. As she bent down and began to lift up Katie, she felt the gun to the back of her head.

"Let her go. You're coming with me." She went to turn, and the guy slammed the gun against her head. She felt the pain and stumbled only for him to strike her in the face and then the stomach before putting her in a headlock, the gun to her head. She realized it was Rosen Armique, and her thoughts were scattered. One, let him take her and then make a move, or two, kill him and who cares if she died. He was the one man she was after. The one who issued the hunt in Cypress, who killed all those soldiers and agents, and killed Evan.

She waited for the opportunity. "Let go of me."

"Not a chance in hell," he said and dragged her from the room. They headed down a different hallway, and soon there were men with him. More gunfire, another explosion. It was a war zone. All she could do was wait to make her move.

* * * *

"Where the fuck is she?" Simon yelled.

"Looks like she rescued Katie, but then someone stopped her," Colonel Brothers said as he looked at the body of Kerrin Bulla.

"Well, he won't be a problem anymore," one of the other Seals said.

"How do you know it was her?" Aqua asked.

He pointed to the gunshot to the head. "April's signature shot." Then they headed toward the door with Colonel Brothers giving orders. "You two get Katie to safety. We're on the hunt for Rosen. He must have April, or Victoria, and if that's the case and April is injured, her chances of living just lessened."

* * * *

It was another twenty minutes before they realized that Rosen and April were gone and so were Victoria and her one guard, Gorbin. Simon took out Fulta.

"Where the fuck did they go?" Aqua asked as they stood around waiting. Colonel Brothers was on the satellite phone as military personnel gathered up prisoners.

"We got them. Let's go," he said, and they hurried to the awaiting jeeps and then made their way through the dark and to another location. It was a small airlift, and the sound of rotors getting started filtered through the air.

"Don't let that chopper take off," Colonel Brothers yelled into the phone. "I got air support on standby, but if they go up, they could crash that thing with April on it."

"Look!" One of the Seals pointed, and Caden, Simon, and Aqua looked. Simon could see April fighting and then Rosen releasing her. The other woman, Victoria, came at her with a knife as they sped faster to get there. They watched as April took a hit but then countered, grabbed the knife, and slit Victoria's throat. Rosen had a gun on her. He was ordering her to get onto the helicopter when she charged at him. The gun went off. They saw her get hit as the jeep came to a halt. They jumped out, and Caden, Simon, and Aqua shot at Rosen and the other guard, killing them.

"April!" Caden yelled. They got to the helipad, and the other men took out the pilot and then ensured they were safe. She was blinking her eyes open. There was a cut on her forehead, her lip was slit open, her cheek bruised, and she was bleeding from her arm.

"She was shot," Aqua said.

"What are you doing here?" she asked.

"Let's get her out of here and to air support. We need to move," Brothers said, and they quickly gathered her up with her moaning and actually bitching about them being there.

When they got her into the jeep with Colonel Brothers driving as they looked over her injuries, she had fire in her green eyes. "Are you guys okay? Why are you here? Are you out of your minds? You could have been killed." She ranted, and Colonel Brothers chuckled. She grimaced as she tried to move.

"Lay the fuck still. Spy or not, you're shot, have been drugged, beaten, and are wearing a see-through fucking outfit. Let us take care of you and get you home," Simon yelled at her.

She squinted and ground her teeth. "Brothers, I'll get you for this."

"I just ask one thing, sweetheart."

"What's that?" she replied to Colonel Brothers.

"I get invited to the wedding."

Epilogue

April lay in bed not wanting to see or talk to anyone. She knew that Mike was pulling through and even gained consciousness. Katie was by his side and had been debriefed on what she could say and reveal about the operation, and considering that she was unconscious when April saved her from getting raped, she didn't know anything about April being there or being a spy.

She decided to rest up and heal, the gunshot a flesh wound that needed twenty-some stitches, and everything else would heal with rest and time. Amelia came by and thanked her for everything she did for her to save her life, twice. She was sworn to secrecy as her men were.

April was still angry with Pierre and Colonel Brothers for informing the men about who she was, and even allowing them to participate in the mission to rescue her and Katie and take out the terrorists. She told them she didn't want rescuing anyway, and didn't even reply to Aqua's comments about her capabilities and the things they would need to talk about. She had a heavy heart. They were coming by here and there but respected her request that she wanted to be alone to process everything and heal. That she hadn't wanted them involved because it was dangerous and it was her profession, her case, and they shouldn't have been brought in. They were angry, but she wasn't budging. She could tell by the way they looked at her that they thought of her differently. Maybe like most men in the field who saw her in action or heard of her capabilities, they felt inferior or like they needed to prove their manliness. She wasn't sure, and analyzing what she thought they were thinking and feeling was giving her another migraine. In fact, she needed some ibuprofen. She moaned a little as she got out of bed. She grabbed what she could find last night after her shower and wound up in a T-shirt that belonged to Caden. She inhaled as she walked to the bathroom, took care of business, then looked at herself in the mirror. She looked like shit. She brushed her teeth, washed up, moaning every time she felt her fingers against her lip and cheek, and then exhaled. She lifted her sleeve to check the stitches and bandage, and her arm felt horrible. She needed to venture into the kitchen for painkillers, but then she heard someone enter her bedroom.

"Aril?" Caden said her name, and she held on to the sink.

"Hey, baby, what are you doing out of bed?" He slid his arm around her waist. She wanted to resist the feel of him, but truth was, just a hug, a kiss, and their presence and she felt better. It was confusing.

"Come on. Maybe have something to eat and then take some painkillers. Simon and Aqua are making some lunch."

She knew she should eat, so she let him walk with her out of the room. When she entered, sure enough, the guys were making sandwiches, and Aqua was chopping up chicken so she would be able to eat something soft because of her busted lip. The sunlight shone through, and she looked toward the ocean view and took a deep breath.

"Maybe have lunch outside today?" Caden suggested."

"Maybe."

She walked toward the counter, and Simon cupped her good cheek so he could look at her lip and the bad cheek.

"More ice later," he said, and she nodded. "I made more chicken salad since that went down easier yesterday for you."

"I appreciate this. You don't need to do this. I can fend for myself. I usually do."

She walked to the refrigerator, took out the pitcher of ice tea, and then placed it down. She felt weak. "Let me do that," Simon said.

She exhaled.

"Things are different now, April. The past you had no one. We're here now, and nothing has changed," Caden said to her.

"Everything has changed. This won't work. There's no need for you to try and act like none of it bothers you. That you don't look at me the same way anymore knowing my capabilities and about my real profession. I get it. That's why no relationship could ever work. I closed off my heart years ago, so just leave it be and move on," she said and then went to turn away, but Caden grabbed her. He lifted her up onto the island, and she straddled his hips. "Caden.

He cupped her good cheek and her hair with one hand and her shoulder with the other. "No. Everything you say is fucking bullshit. You're scared. Scared to love us, to admit that to us, and to let us in, but we do love you. We want you and want to understand and to know who you are, what you really like and dislike. There's no need to hide, to pretend anymore, baby. We know you're a fucking spy, and we still love you and want you. Yes, it is going to be tough worrying about you, but fuck if I care. If we care. We never thought we would fall in love or find a woman to complete us, and you do, damn it. You do." He pressed his lips to her forehead away from the bruising. His words shocked her, and then he hugged her to him. Simon and Aqua joined them. They caressed her back and her arm. She looked at them as tears fell.

"We aren't going anywhere. We know about Evan, and if he lived, baby, he would be here loving you with us," Aqua said. Her eyes widened.

"He was part of our team. He had been out on injury, and his first job back was with a different group because of his capabilities. He died, but you saved the rest of the team and Colonel Brothers. We were meant to find you, to love you, and to make you our woman," Aqua told her.

"So suck it up, pull down those walls around that heart like we're fucking doing being all vulnerable and shit, and let us love you, while you love us right back," Simon stated.

The tears flowed, and she felt like maybe just maybe could do this with them. "I don't want to be alone. I don't want to have to be tough and strong all the time"

"You don't have to be with us. We'll work it all out. We love you forever, baby. You're it for us," Caden said.

"I love you three, too. I do, and I'm scared, and I know I'm going to piss you off and push you away when I feel too vulnerable, but I do love you."

"We'll deal with it military style," Simon said.

"What?" she asked.

"Nothing a firm hand can't resolve," Aqua said and gave her a squeeze.

She chuckled. "I think we should eat outside."

"Okay, but then back to bed to rest," Aqua said as Caden slowly lowered her feet back onto the floor.

She looked over her shoulder as she headed toward the patio. "Not alone though. The three of you right there with me."

"Hell yeah," Simon said and winked.

"Finally," Aqua said, and then they laughed.

"Be ready, baby. If you dish out orders, you better be ready to receive them," Caden told her.

"Oh, I'm more than ready, Chief. More than ready," she said.

They quickly made their lunch and gathered around her outside on the patio with a view of the ocean and thoughts of a future with these three Seals. She didn't want to think about work, about what would be next when she healed, and she didn't want to think about all the ways this could fail. She loved them, and they loved her. They spoke about the future, and Caden's words stating that she was it for them always and forever made her heart soar and her spirits rise. Perhaps finding love, learning to love again, and being in love with these three Seals was the best mission of her life, and maybe even her last. *No way. I love this job too much, Maybe just some little changes, and not so much danger.* After all, she remembered her words to Pierre. *I don't pick the missions. The missions pick me.*

THE END

WWW.DIXIELYNNDWYER.COM

Siren Publishing, Inc.
www.SirenPublishing.com

Lightning Source UK Ltd.
Milton Keynes UK
UKHW02f2355121018
330460UK00013B/1162/P